T0157332

Easing
DISTRACTIONS

Easing DISTRACTIONS

GABRIELLE F. CULMER

This is a work of fiction. All of the characters, names, incidents, organizations, and dialogue in this novel are either the products of the author's imagination or are used fictitiously.

Archway Publishing books may be ordered through booksellers or by contacting:

Archway Publishing
1663 Liberty Drive
Bloomington, IN 47403
www.archwaypublishing.com
1 (888) 242-5904

Author photo credit: David Beyda Photography.

ISBN: 978-1-4808-8179-2 (sc)
ISBN: 978-1-4808-8178-5 (e)

Library of Congress Control Number: 2019913006

Print information available on the last page.

Archway Publishing rev. date: 9/16/2019

Contents

Prologue

Many happy years were spent at 34 Beneville Road. Margaux became an expert at entertaining while pursuing her practice in the heart of Knightsbridge. Nicholas was the perfect father and a source of strength in the early years when Margaux was a socialite with a medical profession and balanced both those facets of her life. Her father was an ambassador and French aristocrat who marvelled at all her accomplishments. The home had belonged to her family, along with other property in the Loire Valley and the South of France. Holidays were spent between the ancestral homes of both parents.

Margaux's untimely passing changed the lives of those who loved and knew her. She was still young and had been stricken by an aneurysm. Amelie was at university and in a budding romance with Lars, while her only son, Hank, was just in his first position as a trader in the city. Nothing about Margaux was lost as she had contributed so much to their lives and to the lives of those closest to her, including her sister, Marguerite, who became a second parent to them. She continued all the traditions and kept the memories alive.

One New Year's Eve, just before Amelie was due to be married, there had been an attempted heist of their works of art worth millions.

Her mother's identity had been stolen and her documents used to convey a sale. Luckily, it was caught before the art had been sold. However, Amelie had presumably been the victim of a crime as she had been watched and targeted. She was able to overcome the trauma, surrounded by family and friends. Now the culprits are in prison and are due to be released.

Margaux did not elaborate on her business dealings to Nicholas and kept them in her family. She was a devoted wife and mother who found the joie de vivre in any event. Her bursting personality affected all who knew her, including those from the past. She had a sense of style and was often in the fashion columns for her influence. She was also a part-time buyer for her mother-in-law's boutique and had arranged the influence of designers to tropical locations with the import of their collections. In her day, this increased her popularity. She exhibited this savoir faire across the globe during luxurious travel for social events and family vacations. To the present day, during events, her presence can be felt. It has shaped Amelie into who she has become. Margaux's achievements are prevalent throughout *Easing Distractions*.

Chapter 1

Saturday in Knightsbridge

*A*melie-Aurore awoke refreshed and enthusiastic, ensconced in her sheets and duvet and surrounded by her duck-shell-blue bedroom. The bay windows spanned the interior and overlooked the plush green back garden of her house at 34 Beneville Road, where the spring tulips, vinca minor periwinkles, and azaleas bloomed. She and Lars had decided to stay in Knightsbridge, to which she was accustomed.

She now owned a property consultancy and sustainable lifestyle firm, and he had become the senior partner of his legal practice. Married life had changed her, yet much remained the same. Nicholas, her father; her grandparents; and her brother, Hank Mullbury, were still a part of her foundation. However, her closest adviser was Lars. Her aunt Marguerite and uncle Lance were in the French countryside, while Amelie's residence in Bermuda awaited their summer retreat.

The couple had married three years ago. It had been three years of wedded bliss with all the legal issues now behind her. They enjoyed parties and the summer seasons together at the regatta and at the tennis and polo matches, and late summers visiting France and Bermuda.

Amelie's property consulting office was near Sloane Square, to which she had a short commute. She remained in the environment in which she'd been raised.

It was a beautiful summer morning, hot and sweltering. She felt the heat rise to her second-floor bedroom. Lars had a study in the basement, which was the coolest place this time of the year. She enjoyed a lazy Saturday lie-in and awaited his return from Gibraltar on business. She checked her phone and saw his text. He was on his way from the airport.

Fabulous, she thought as she clambered down the stairs to check on brunch. Marietta was in the kitchen, busily preparing Lars's favourite of salmon and eggs. Amelie inhaled the aroma of freshly baked croissants. "Good morning. It smells lovely," said Amelie.

"Good morning. Thank you. I have made some fresh croissants. What time is Lars arriving?"

"He should be here in about an hour, so there is still time to get it all ready. I will be dressing upstairs. Let him know if he arrives while I am up there," replied Amelie.

"Sure. The food will be ready by then."

"Thank you. I'll be down soon. I am heading up now."

Amelie climbed the stairs to her boudoir and picked out a superb outfit to greet Lars. The phone rang. It was her father, Nicholas, with perfect timing.

"Hello, dear. How are you?"

"Hello, Dad. Just great. How are you?"

"Just fine. Nadia and I are arriving next week in London from Guernsey. The week after we are getting a head start to the summer on the island. I hope that you will join us in August."

"Sure. We're absolutely planning on it. Then we will see Auntie in France. Lars is arriving from his business trip, and I am getting ready."

"I see. Sorry to bother you. Well, Hank is meeting us next week for lunch. Would you like to join us in Mayfair?"

"Sure. That would be lovely as always. I will see if Lars is free and get back to you. Safe travels, and see you soon."

"Bye, dear. See you soon."

Her father had retired and was content spending a few months of each year at home on the island to see his parents, who were still active. Winifred still managed to do the shopping, and her staff always loyally supported her. She held the planning of Amelie's wedding in such esteem and was excited about everyone joining them in August. It was still a few weeks away, and Amelie still had events in London that she had to attend before she and Lars took off. She also had work mounting that had to be delegated to her staff.

She attended the usual flower shows, tennis matches, regattas, balls, polo matches, horse trials, and concerts. Later in the summer, she and Lars were usually off to see her grandparents and spent the end of the summer visiting her aunt. There was work from sales and public relations she had to complete, and then they would enjoy a perfect summer basking in the sun and visiting the house in the countryside. She enjoyed rural walks with Lars and her niece and nephew, Hannah and Jasper, at weekends. Memories of her youth with Hank and Margaux conjured in her mind.

It was a name she had not thought about for some time, her mother's. Having been married for two years, she found that time had swept by so quickly. She was absorbed in married bliss and the prospect of having someone always there and her new life. She had known Lars since university; however, they had turned over a new leaf on their wedding day. Close friends and family flew in and witnessed her and Lars exchanging vows on a tropical island. The guests all danced until the early morning, overlooking the beach from the patio—the patio where memories prevailed of her youth and parties with her parents. Then was a real wedding celebration, the event of her life. It was true that she felt nervous, and it was to be expected. But initially she had the guiding arms of her father to whisk her down the aisle while Lars waited at the end. Nicholas had been her pillar throughout her mother's death and her relationship. He lived in Guernsey, but with a flat in Mayfair, he was able to see her regularly with his new fiancée.

This was the fabric of Amelie's life. It was not as settled as she had hoped, what with the new business and Lars having to work around the world from time to time. It was an ideal life to live. It was filled with substance: family, work, friends, and love. She would not exchange it for anything.

Amelie finally got dressed and headed to the kitchen to oversee the buffet. Marietta had set the mahogany table in the dining room and placed the meal on the buffet.

"Thank you. It smells marvellous. He has texted and is around the corner. He should be here any minute."

"Perfect. It is all ready for him," Marietta replied, having perfected her language skills.

"I think that I hear a door slam. That must be him. I'll be right back," said Amelie.

She rushed to the front door as she had done every month to welcome her husband back from some business venture. She opened the door. "Darling, so wonderful to see you," she said, greeting Lars with a hug and kiss.

"Thank you. Wonderful to see you too. It has been quite a journey this time. You look amazing and ... my, something smells delicious," he commented as he dragged his bags into the foyer.

"Yes, Marietta has made brunch. Hope that you are hungry, dear."

"Yes, famished," he admitted, although he'd been served what he thought was a meagre meal on the flight. "I can eat something."

"Fabulous. Once you have freshened up, meet me downstairs in the dining room, where I'll be waiting."

"See you in a bit."

They enjoyed a quiet Saturday morning brunch. Amelie served more eggs and fresh croissants to him. Lars Faverer was now an equity partner at the law firm and had meetings and commitments lined up that week.

"Anything interesting coming up?" Amelie asked.

"Yes. More wheeling and dealing. I have a trip to Malta again in two weeks."

Amelie looked despondent as she remembered the ordeal the last time he had visited and what she'd been through. He was away when the initial crime occurred and her mother's documents disappeared from the deposit box. The case seemed to be closed, and those responsible for the identity theft of her mother, Margaux, had been put to justice. But so many questions remained unanswered, such as how it had all happened. How had the thieves received the key to the deposit box? Where had she lost hers? Why did they target her, and how did they know where she was located? It all remained a mystery. Would they strike again?

She healed because of the quick legal process and her sturdy family life. It was mostly due to the support of Lars, Hank, Nicholas, and her father-in-law, Dixon. She had the reclusive atmosphere of Lionel and Winifred's home on the island and Lars beside her the whole time. Also, refuge with her aunt. The chateau in France was beautiful in the summer with its surrounding gardens and mystical exterior. Her aunt Marguerite was recovering from what seemed like the re-emergence of her late sister's memory on New Year's Eve by the culprits. There was a resurgence of memories that had been drowned. Amelie had received the help that she needed and found it difficult to face the reality of her nerves at twenty-eight. Still, she beavered on and found a new and secure environment in which to work, which seemed the perfect anecdote for victims of crime. Her office was located near Sloane Square, a stone's throw from the flat. She'd started the business shortly after her honeymoon. Clarence, her former boss, was disappointed when she left, but she knew that after the ordeal, she wanted more control of her movements and who had access to her. She now dealt with affluent clients, and thanks to her reputation and family connections—in particular Hank's—she had a growing client list. She found property and accommodation for clients around Great Britain and worked weekends at their country retreat in Gloucestershire. Her close friend Lydia and her husband, Manny, also spent weekends with them in the countryside. They looked forward to the summer with the horses and trekking along country paths on foot.

Amelie's and Lars's was an unconventional honeymoon. They'd backpacked in South America and had an eco-friendly accommodation and visit to a remote part of Eleuthera. Nights were spent along the main highway passing through quaint towns and watching the sunset. She also cherished the time in the Loire Valley and reminisced about her childhood and thought about her new life with Lars. Memories of Margaux abounded, and Amelie only wished that she had been at the wedding. From a practical point of view, those days were gone, and she had new memories to make with Lars.

They finished their meal and decided to go to the shops and the gym that afternoon. There was an energy in Chelsea that she knew well. It always reeled her in as a local.

"All right then, are we ready?" Lars asked as he took his gym bag from the Rover.

"Yep, ready as I'll ever be. I am thrilled that you made it back in time today."

"Thanks, darling. I had an early start though. But there is nothing better than more time with you, dear."

"Thanks. Same here. Marietta, we are off. See you later," Amelie called out.

They hopped in the four-wheel drive and set out initially for the gym.

"Right then. Nicholas called and wants to meet with Hank for lunch next week. Are you interested?"

"Sure. Just get back to me with the time and the day. I am actually looking forward to seeing him. I must warn you, it is not good news about the case. Roger has filled me in a bit."

"Are you certain? Things should be more sorted, right?" she asked.

"Yes, dear. However, I will let Nicholas fill you in. I really have to wait before I can get involved."

"Good heavens. OK, I will wait. Let's change the subject and not ruin my Saturday entirely," she responded, annoyed.

They drove up to the gym's entrance and parked the car. The afternoon session was gruelling for Lars, who had been away all week. The hotel gyms were adequate for a certain period of time. After the workout, they sat and sipped fresh energy drinks before heading to the shops. It was an outing that they enjoyed while they could. It was a crowded and sunny yet crisp afternoon. The atmosphere was energetic with people in the neighbourhood also celebrating the weekend.

Marietta assisted the couple while they unloaded the car with the packages. She would rather have gone herself as there was always more that she needed to prepare meals.

"Thanks for that," Lars said as he closed the vehicle.

"You are welcome. I need to check that you have everything."

"Sure, indeed," he responded, knowing that she would find something, being a professional cook.

"What are we doing later? What is there on Netflix? Why don't we watch a film?" asked Amelie.

"Great idea. And then I need to go over my notes of the trip for Monday."

"Sure, but you can spend some time at least until dinner. Marietta is making your favourite."

"Certainly, dear."

Nicholas had arrived early at the Game in Mayfair, their favourite restaurant. Amelie had been pesce-vegetarian for some time but would enjoy the odd meal with her family. It was a healthy lifestyle that she was trying to maintain before starting a family.

"Father, how are you?" she greeted warmly.

"Wonderful, dear, just wonderful. How are you?"

"Great. We got a new client today. He is an entrepreneur who needs luxury and sustainable management services. He travels all over the world and needs someone to organise his routine, whether New York, Tokyo, or London."

"Fabulous. I am so proud of you. I am sure that he will be pleased with your suggestions."

It was a leap for Amelie to go out on her own and provide management services. She had managed to set her clients up in the best parts of London and elsewhere in Europe. Now she was going international. She provided connections to anything they wanted to maintain their luxury lifestyles. It was easier said than done.

Nicholas gave much entrepreneurial advice and could refer a few old clients, but Amelie was growing the business from her own intuition. Her market was a newer niche than his former clientele. He did the odd consulting, but she had a younger, more vibrant crowd into eco-tourism and adventure, as well as top-of-the-line travel arrangements. It was a talent she had acquired from being in society as the granddaughter of a French aristocrat and diplomat. She had been accustomed to the luxurious side of life by her grandfather, who was known for his entertainment in Mayfair and his debonair and sophisticated manner.

Hank walked in with his lengthy and confident stride. "Sorry. Am I late? I tried to get here on time. Hello, Father, Amelie," he announced as he greeted them both. "Jenny sends her apologies. Hannah has a bug, and she is nursing her. Is Lars on his way?"

"Yes. He should be here any minute," Amelie responded.

"Good. Father, how was your trip?"

"Marvellous. Nadia should be here tomorrow. We have the tennis, regattas, and races this year, you know."

"As you do every year. We shall be at the regatta. What about you, Amelie?"

"Definitely. I also want to catch some tennis and some polo later on."

"Fabulous." Hank looked at his father.

"Now, Amelie, it is not very good news coming from France."

"The culprits will soon be released for the fraud. The ringleader has not been found, it has been revealed. They were working for the main individual, someone a bit closer to here. Do not get over fraught about this. We shall have this all sorted. Provided the criminals do not step foot in the UK. I am sure you understand."

"I think that this is horrible. First, I cannot be certain that I am safe when they are free, as we do not know how we were targeted by these criminals. Also, the thought that there was someone else is worrying. It is a mystery as to who that could be and why the person targeted us," she confided.

"We know, we know. We feel the same. However, they will not be allowed here. Roger at the law firm has made sure of that. As for the ringleader, he is probably in hiding. It was a major heist attempt.

Thirty million pounds worth of Renaissance art from the chateau. We have taken very many precautions since then. Everything is now digitised and password-protected. So there is no question: it can't happen again. Remember the advice we were given?" Nicholas reassured her.

"I know, it's just that we have been through so much, and two years seems like such a short time to serve. How annoying—just when I have so much to look forward to this summer and am getting my life together."

Lars walked in hurriedly and approached the table. "Hello. Hello. Sorry that I am late. We had a meeting this morning that ran over. Nicholas, so wonderful to see you. How have you been? Hank, how are you?"

"Fine. Fine," Nicholas answered, with Hank motioning in agreement and giving a handshake. "Not to worry, we have not ordered. We were just updating Amelie on the case. It has been some time, but we seem to be resurfacing a few issues," he continued despondently.

"Oh, I see. Sorry to hear that. Poor dear. Don't worry, Roger is working on it," he reassured her.

"So how was Malta? I hear that you have just returned?" asked Hank, changing the subject.

"Yes. It was fabulous. We got so much work done. It is always the case with that client account. What about you? I see that a new IPO is on the horizon?"

"That is right. The new company is selling shares. If you are interested, the returns should be high."

"Well, fill me in later. We will see what we can buy," promised Lars.

"So are we all set on what we want? We have been here numerous times," said Nicholas.

"Not really. Not much of an appetite. Just a shrimp and avocado salad for me," responded Amelie.

"Cheer up, dear. We'll have a superb summer with weekends in the country and then down to see your nan. You'll see," comforted Lars.

The meals arrived swiftly. Afterwards, they all sipped coffee while commiserating over the prospect of reliving the ordeal. Hank and Lars had to rush back to work, while Amelie lingered a bit longer before heading back to work. After all, she had to remain balanced so that she could cater to her clients.

When back at Sloane Square, she ensconced herself in her small office. Delianna brought her usual afternoon almond latte.

"Thanks, Delianna. Has Mr Mitchvale responded?"

"Yes. He says that he will call you this afternoon. He has a big trip approaching that needs some planning."

"Perfect. Send it right through then."

She sipped her coffee and went over ideal prospects in London and Zurich. She wanted to impress him deeply. She still had a nagging feeling and wanted to put it all out of her mind.

Winifred and Lionel relaxed and sipped tea on the wicker settee on the veranda. The temperature had cooled and was not sweltering. Verena was clearing up the dining room after dinner, while Rema put away the last of the ironing.

"Soon the house will be full. Nicholas and the children are coming in August," Winifred reminded Lionel.

"Yes. As usual we will have a full house. It seems as though they just left."

"It certainly does. I am very thrilled to see Amelie so happy. Meanwhile, we have a relaxing few months ahead of us. I love how the palm trees rustle in the sea breeze. And my hibiscus and poinsettias have bloomed. The night jasmine is about to blossom. Being here, I appreciate all the small things in life. Do you remember our luxurious trips to Hong Kong, London, Paris, Venice, and New York? Now it is much more convenient to travel. When I was a child, we had steamships at first from London—and then flights. Do you remember when we travelled on the Concorde and the romantic trips on the gondolas and on the Orient Express?"

"I sure do. Those were the days. Now all that we have is what we wished, a life of tranquillity with a happy family," he responded.

"It was not always this way after the sudden death of Margaux. My poor grandchildren. What I would have given just to have her back."

"I know, dear, I know. What we all would have given. Amelie has turned over a new leaf and is settled in her new life."

"That is just wonderful. I cannot wait to see them," she admitted. Winifred was a very shrewd and fashionable woman on the island. She was once a boutique owner and had travelled to New York, London, and Paris as a buyer for her designer evening wear business. She was crafty with shipping and customs exchange because she'd had to bring in merchandise. She was also very aware of her market and what was in demand for the fashionable woman living in a remote location. Travel was essential, and while customers were able to shop abroad, it was not always convenient to do so. Winifred had been raised in the UK and descended from a long history of islanders. Lionel was also raised in the UK, having arrived with his family on the island as a child. His family made their fortune in the hospitality business and had a small chain near seaside villages across the UK.

Winifred's history on the island dated back to the eighteenth century and was filled with war heroes and statesmen. Her influence was strong when it came to appearance as the public valued her opinion. She was practical and had a strong work ethic as a business owner for over thirty years. She had sold the business, and the brand now created its own leisure line popular with most tourists on the island.

She entertained on a large scale annually and hosted enviable soirées in their gated community to which the "who's who" and up-and-coming of the island would be invited, all of them arriving fashionably dressed.

"I have to make sure that the boat is checked out before they arrive. Nicholas loves the boat," Lionel said.

"Always did. We could never get him away from it. I was always so frantic that something might happen to him."

"It never did though …"

She had helped to raise Amelie and Hank after the passing of Margaux. She was also grateful to their aunt Marguerite, who spent her time at Vicomte Manor in Surrey, named after an area of her favourite island retreat and the chateaux in the Loire Valley where they were partially raised as children. This influenced Amelie as she would spend holidays in France with continental exposure.

Marguerite and Lance had been at the chateau in the Loire Valley all spring. She was due back in London to enjoy the summer season until the family visited. It was slightly crisp, and she only needed a light jacket for their early morning walk in the valley and along the vineyards.

She had heard the news from her lawyer and was despondent at the outcome. "I hope that Amelie will be OK. She is all that I worry about, especially since we lost Margaux. This news will not come easy, so it is best we get back to London as soon as we can."

"I agree," responded Lance. "She had been doing so well, and now this again." He was just as concerned about her as if she were their child, one that they had never managed to have. Marguerite and Margaux had been socialites in Knightsbridge because of their family background, and Marguerite had left it too late before she thought about marriage and children. She knew how fragile Amelie could be under pressure, and she was concerned that Amelie and Lars would be targets if they were in a place where the culprits could find them. Amelie would be safer back at Vicomte Manor, where Marguerite hosted tea parties and croquet matches on the lawn with Lance. Lance was an equestrian, and this was the season to return to the country.

Their walk drew them closer to the chateau which was overwhelming in stature among the trees. The front door was solid oak with brass handles, and a long foyer welcomed them. They headed to the breakfast room and sat down to a French country breakfast with fresh eggs, fruit from the garden, and home-made croissants prepared by Anne, the cook. Lance felt a slight chill and shrugged it off as being a bit under the weather.

"What is the matter, dear?"

"Oh, I am a bit queasy, and there is a chill. I must be coming down with something."

"Let me feel your forehead to see if you have a temperature." She placed her hand on his forehead.

"A bit warm. Perhaps you should go lie down."

"I'm all right. It will pass, I am sure. I will have an aspirin," he promised.

"Right then. Have some hot tea," she offered as she passed the teapot.

"Thanks. I am sure it will be fine, though, dear. I have some work to do and will rest later."

The chateau still had fireplaces. She thought that maybe it was a bit chilly for him since they had stopped the heating.

"Yes. I think that we should leave soon and get back to the countryside."

"Whatever you wish, dear," he responded.

Marguerite spent the remainder of the day in her dressing room picking out outfits suitable for the summer season. It would be filled with warm eventful afternoons in the countryside or by the shoreline, and then she would return to the South of France with the family. She assessed what would fit in the suitcases and packed.

Chapter 2

Periwinkles in Bloom

May was always a nostalgic month for Amelie. There were the memories of studying for finals and the shaping of the past year, continuing with a summer filled with family and friends. She sat on her settee and reflected on what had been achieved. The sun beat on the pavements as she surveyed the passers-by through the bay windows of her childhood home at 34 Beneville Road. It was also Nicholas's birthday month, followed by flower shows, proms, Hyde Park concerts, and theatrical performances.

She and Lars were to spend the weekend in the countryside. Her horses Velvet and Polka were being readied by the stable attendant, Nestor. This was the best place to be at the moment, a place where she could breathe easily and bask in the spring sunshine. It was almost 6 p.m. Lars was due to arrive at any moment.

He pulled up and entered the flat. "Hello, dear. Have you been waiting long?"

"No, not at all. I am just gathering my thoughts."

"Sorry. I tried to get out early so that we could get down there before the traffic."

"What about a nice meal at the pub near Oxfordshire on the way down?"

"Sounds perfect. I won't be able to drink," he responded. He was a stickler for regulations and very responsible.

"I know why I married you," she responded.

"Right. I am just going to pop upstairs, and then I will be right down."

"I'll be waiting." Amelie had only packed the essentials. The converted barn was perfectly equipped for them on weekends. She looked forward to country rides and walks to the town. The fresh spring air would clear her thoughts for the long bank holiday weekend.

The couple drove, listening to their favourite tunes until the Fanfare Arms. They were delighted at the crowds and found a cosy table nestled near the back window.

"I'll just get some drinks, and then we can order," Lars offered, inclining his head towards the bar.

"Thanks, dear. Just the usual for me."

"Got it." He knew that meant a glass of house red with roast chicken.

Amelie checked her messages while she waited for him to return with the drinks.

"Right then. The food should be here in a bit. Here is your wine." He passed her the glass.

"Thank you. I could really use this today. I am still bothered from our meeting with Dad."

"I know. Try to keep your mind off that. What I can tell you is that Kexan Shadrock and Tom Mesnel are out this October. They suspect a third person as the ringleader of the gang. They have done it before. And another heist occurred while they were in prison in Brussels. Therefore, there is still someone out there who assisted. Unfortunately, we do not know who that person might be or where he might be."

"Can we hire an investigator to find out?" she asked.

"That would be fine, but I do not know if it is advisable. It is police business. I am sure that they have some sort of lead, which is why the operation is so confidential."

"I understand. We'll just wait until we hear more," she said mechanically.

"Sorry. We need to play by the rules. It worked the last time. Roger can fill you in more. That is just the overall consensus."

"Thanks, dear. I really do appreciate it. That being the case, I suppose I should just be vigilant."

"Yes, while keeping ourselves safe, especially when thieves are out of jail and we are travelling abroad. The paintings are still valuable to them."

"I know. They are safely tucked away at the gallery on display. I no longer feel safe with them out there."

"Perhaps you should talk it over with Marguerite and Hank and they can see what can be done," he suggested.

The waitress brought the food, which was flavoured with and rosemary and enhanced by fresh farm produce.

"It smells delicious. Thank you," Amelie commented.

"Yes. It does smell delicious. I am happy that I ordered the same."

"Great. I am tucking in."

The couple stayed a short while before driving another hour to Gloucestershire. They pulled up at the stately home, now owned by Hank from his father, and passed by to their wedding gift, the converted barn. They stopped and unloaded the Rover and then walked up the path to the idyllic country doorstep surrounded with pink azaleas, vinca minor periwinkles, bluebells, and honeysuckles.

"It is so cosy," Amelie said as she walked in, still smelling the flowers at the door. "Look at the dining table all set."

"Nestor must have been expecting us earlier."

"It is lovely though. So quaint," she observed as she plopped her bags down in the living room.

"I'll just take these to the back."

The master bedroom was decorated with wood panelling on the walls and cream-coloured rugs on the floor. Amelie had decorated it just before the wedding, and it had a very clean country feel. She loved the contrast between the rustic look and the urban cream from Knightsbridge. She had remodelled the kitchen, and it had all the modern amenities to entertain during the weekends when the full family were on the premises.

"Another glass of wine, dear? We still have more Argentinian Malbec," offered Lars.

"Perfect. We can drop down right here on the sofa. What *is* on the news, I wonder?" She flicked through the channels.

"I have found a cherry chocolate cake in the fridge. Nestor must have brought it from town. Do you wish for any?"

"Sure. Superb."

They nestled into their happy Friday night in and laughed and talked until the early hours as if back at university. They finally fell asleep, looking forward to a long ride out the following day.

The following morning Lars treated Amelie to a full breakfast with flowers from the garden displayed on the table. Amelie cut through the thick-crusted home-made loaf and poured the fresh milk into her coffee.

"Thanks, darling. I really appreciate this. I did not hear when you got up, though."

"No. I wanted to surprise you. Besides, I wanted to make sure that the horses were ready for our ride today."

"Perfect. It tastes delicious, dear," she replied, chuffed.

"Thank you." He was flattered and leant over for a kiss, which she obligingly returned.

"I am so full," she admitted as she took a sip of the freshly squeezed orange juice. "The fruit is so succulent here," she remarked as she bit into a pear.

"I am glad that you like it," he said, bemused.

"This is just brilliant, but I have to stop and get ready. I can't wait to see the horses."

The ground was now thawed. It had been a brutal winter, which Amelie spent mostly in London with full heating. It was perfect spring weather to spend with the horses, who had been brushed and prepared that morning.

Amelie mounted Polka while Lars took Velvet. They rode down a cut-out path on the large estate. They started with an easy walk as they took in the crisp morning air.

"Would you look at the bluebells?" she commented.

"I know, perfect this time of the year. Superb. I feel so refreshed. I don't see why we don't do this more often."

"We can now that the weather is better. I fancy spending more time here. We have been doing the London thing for so long—since university."

"True. I have no qualms about spending more time here. I must admit, we have some more to do at the house."

"Yes. We still have to refurbish the guest bathroom and the wash-room, I suppose."

"Not to worry. All in good time, dear," he reassured her.

They had been riding for half an hour up steep hills and down the path, ducking branches and seeing tiny deer and foxes.

"Right, I think that I am out of shape," she admitted as they got to the clearing of a vast field.

"I'll race you to the top," he challenged her, and broke into a canter.

"OK," she said, facing the challenge. They both charged for the next ten minutes until utterly exhausted.

"I think that I will be sore for weeks. That was so exhilarating. I really needed that," she commented.

"I know. So did I. Took the pressure off," he admitted as he dismounted and took off his riding helmet.

They patted the horses and strode arm in arm back to the cottage.

"I want to go to town later and get Dad that tweed jacket for his birthday."

"Anything you want, dear."

The couple enjoyed the rest of the day cooking and running errands in town. They received friendly waves as they popped into shops for their items. It had always been a home away from home for Amelie and for Lars, who had been raised in Reading and who had known Amelie now for ten years.

Nicholas was celebrating his birthday the second week of May. The family were to gather at his flat in Mayfair and then have a meal at a swanky restaurant in the same town.

"How do I look?" Amelie asked.

"Smashing. Absolutely smashing."

"Thank you." She wore a black lace top covered by a sheer long-sleeved cardigan with a relaxed pair of black silk trousers and a silver chain belt. "Might be a bit muggy out tonight."

"I think so." Lars was fitted in a coat and tie for the occasion.

"We had better leave. Have we got the gift?" she asked.

"Here, dear. No need to worry."

"Brilliant. Let's go."

Hank, Jennifer, Jasper, and Hannah were already in the living room, speaking to Nicholas and Nadia. Hank and Nicholas were embroiled in a discussion over the value of the pound and its effect on the stock exchange. The last few months had made it difficult for him at the brokerage firm. Nicholas was merely in consultancy after having made his fortune in the business.

"Jenny, are the children going to camp this summer?"

"Not entirely. They will be home in June, and then in July we have somewhere for them. I enjoy having them at home with me. I get so down when school begins again." The children, now five and eight, had a good command of the English language and specially wished their grandfather a happy birthday.

They heard a buzz. Mildred, who had been Amelie's nanny and family housekeeper and had helped to raise her, buzzed up the visitors. Mildred was also a source of strength when Margaux died. Occasions were difficult without her as she was the life of the party.

"Hello. Happy birthday, Daddy," greeted Amelie.

"Yes, happy birthday!" added Lars.

"Thank you. Wonderful to see you. Have a seat. What would you like?"

"I'll get it for you. What would you like? Champagne?" offered Hank.

"Yes. That would be perfect."

"Thank you. That is fine," Lars replied.

"Here is a gift for you, Dad."

"Thank you. I'll put it here. We can open it later. We should head over in a bit."

"Perfect. I'll have the after-dinner drinks and cake ready," commented Mildred.

The party left for dinner and celebrated Nicholas's milestone of sixty years. It was an extremely special occasion to have his children with him instead of at a quiet retreat elsewhere. The champagne was flowing while the children enjoyed Shirley Temples or seltzer and juice. A fine roast was ordered with vegetable dishes on the side. Amelie stuck to mostly vegetarian food with salmon.

Jenny oversaw the children, who were becoming tired and eager for dessert.

"Probably we should not order too much as there is cake back at the house. Mildred is expecting us," suggested Jenny.

"I am sure that it is fine. Order what you wish. We can have two desserts," suggested Nicholas.

They looked at each other and smirked as there was a surprise waiting for him.

Hank and his family were staying in town, and Jenny would take the children home after the cake and ice cream she had promised them.

"Right then. I shall have the white chocolate soufflé," ordered Nadia.

"Sounds lovely. I will have the same," Jenny echoed.

"I think that I will have the cheese platter. Would you like to share?" Amelie asked Lars.

"Sure. What about you, Hank?"

"Just some coffee. And you, Dad?"

"The sorbet. Looks enticing with all those tropical flavours."

"Superb. You had better order then," Nadia suggested.

The party wore on another hour, and then they all set out to return the flat at about nine. When they arrived, the conversations could be heard before they entered.

"Surprise!" someone shouted as Nicholas made his way in.

"Oh my gosh, this is a surprise. I thought that my flat had been invaded."

"Thank you all for coming," Hank said.

"Happy birthday!"

"For he's a jolly good fellow, for he's a jolly good fellow ..." could be heard.

"Happy birthday!"

Nicholas was very surprised. Some of his old friends from his younger working days in London had been invited.

"My, this is fantastic. Thank you all. More champagne? Canapés, anyone?" he offered.

"I have it all sorted," stated Mildred as she and Marietta went around the group of one dozen.

"We could never forget your birthday. It was always a wonderful way to start the season," stated Edward Ferry, Nicholas's colleague from university and from the first investment bank where he had trained.

"Thank you. Jolly good to see you, old chap. My, it has been ages. How are you keeping yourself these days?"

"Very good. I see that your family is growing even more. Are you still consulting Agnes Inc. out in Guernsey?"

"Only on the side now. I am no longer full-time. It makes it easier to travel," admitted Nicholas.

"Surely you have not gone out to pasture just yet, old boy. There is fire in you yet."

"I know, I know. I leave it up to my son now. He is in the profession."

"I see. Well, all right for some, I would imagine."

"That's right. I have not seen some of you in years," Nicholas observed.

"We just wanted to get as many as could fit," joked Lydia, Amelie's childhood friend for twenty years.

"Well, you did a fine job of that," responded Nicholas.

"We know, Dad. We just wanted you to have a soirée to celebrate. We were so excited. We could hardly keep it under wraps."

"I am sure we would have left sooner had I known."

"Of course. But they were well looked after here, wouldn't you say?" she admitted.

"Yes, dear," he agreed. However, he knew that his standard of manners with his friends would have been slightly different. She had good intentions, and that was what counted. Besides, they had known each other for years.

"Well, thank you for coming, Cynthia, and you, Orry. It was lovely seeing you both."

"Happy birthday, Nicholas. When Nadia phoned, we decided we would miss this for the world. There is so much to catch up on. And I hear Amelie and Hank are doing very well," Cynthia noted.

"I know. Such brilliant children I have."

"Yes. I said to Cynthia that we could not miss it. We have not seen you in years. How have you been? We need to keep in touch more often. It is hard with us here and you in Guernsey, but we must try," insisted Orry.

"I know. Where has the time gone? We used to have lunch every week at the club here. We need to start again."

"You just let me know when, and I will look forward to it," Orry responded, pleased.

Mildred took Amelie aside. "Your aunt Marguerite sends her regrets. Lance has not been well, I am afraid. She's looking forward to having you to lunch next weekend with a few friends."

"Thanks. Such a pity. I will phone her anyway. After Dad's birthday, the summer just rolls out."

"That is how time flies," advised Mildred.

The party went on until almost midnight. Nicholas appeared to be in seventh heaven with his old friends and colleagues. It was the happiest that he had been in some time, and it made him more optimistic about the years to come. Laughter could be heard again from his flat, reminiscent of his glory days.

Amelie awoke in a daze, still feeling the euphoria of a successful evening. She had done everything to make her father happy, and he was almost youthful again in his element. It was one of the happiest times since her wedding.

"How delightful it was," she commented to Lars.

"That is an understatement. I did not think that anyone would leave. They certainly know how to have a soirée."

"It is true. Now you see what has influenced me. With Mummy's side, I must be a socialite. She was the belle of Beauchamp at one point."

"I have heard from your aunt. What a lifestyle they had in the area. How wonderful that you have such memories."

Lars's family life was demurer and more conventional. He was from a middle-class Reading background. His was a solid foundation where Alice preferred to stay at home. He'd always been intrigued by Amelie's lifestyle.

"That reminds me. We are having lunch with Auntie next week. Do say that you can make it."

"Sure, I can. I do not travel until the week after."

The drive to Surrey was hectic on a Saturday afternoon. Amelie and Lars waited on the M5 and crawled through traffic. It was some time before they drove up the welcoming driveway of Vicomte Manor, an old country mansion with pillars and a circular driveway ensconced in the idyllic countryside. For Amelie, it was like returning home.

Marguerite was greeting guests as they entered the patio area after having been escorted in by the butler. It was now the third weekend in May, and she was initiating the season in style. Champagne flutes awaited them while the waiters walked around with the appetisers.

Dining tables were set up in tents in the vast garden while a classical pianist played in the background.

Amelie spotted Hank and his family playing croquet on the lawn. Laughter could be heard.

"Darling, I am so happy that you could make it," Marguerite greeted her.

"It is our pleasure. How have you been?"

"Fine, thank you. We got back last week. Lars, so happy that you are here."

"Superb. I wouldn't have missed it. Always such good fun at your parties. How's Lance?"

"He is coming along. He still has a chill and went to the sitting room for a minute, hoping it will pass. He has preliminary tests next week," she disclosed.

"My. I hope that it is not anything serious," replied Amelie, concerned.

"No, we do not think so. It is just a precaution," Marguerite replied, askance.

"We'll just wait then and hope for the best," reassured Amelie.

"Yes, it is all that we can do."

"That is right. Best of luck to him. I'll tell him myself when I see him," said Lars.

"You can go in and see him when you are ready."

"That would be lovely."

It was very unusual for Lance not to be the dedicated entertainer. He was always there as support during the parties. Amelie grew slightly wary of the situation. She remembered how suddenly she'd lost Margaux almost seven years ago now. Could the family be facing the same issue again? She decided to bury her emotions and to get on with mingling a bit before being seen venturing indoors, as she had planned to spend time with her uncle Lance.

It was a bright and breezy spring day. The guests wore summer dresses and blazers and sipped champers and cocktails, basking in the glory of a delightful Saturday afternoon. Lunch was served as guests wandered to the tent to be seated. Lance sat next to Marguerite. Hank and his family joined them. Amelie and Lars entertained the second table in Marguerite's absence until the dessert and coffee were served.

"How are you feeling?" asked Hank.

"A bit better. The doctors will find out what is wrong eventually."

"There is always something, isn't there?" he reasoned.

"Absolutely. We'll get to the bottom of it, and then I'll be back in true form to finish the summer activities," promised Lance.

"I am sure. We are all looking forward to having you back in top form," Hank encouraged him.

"Yes. You will see, darling. We will complete the summer, and before we know it, we will be entertaining everyone in France," Marguerite reassured him.

His mood was lightened by those around him, and he wanted to believe that what they'd said was true.

After coffee, Amelie and Lars joined their table and discussed more plans. Amelie was eager for the regatta and the charity gala in Cannes. She was also keen on the tennis and seeing some equestrian trials. Lars was keen on the polo and museum events when he was not working.

"Uncle, we are so pleased that you made it out. It is a bit nippy, but the sun will be out again," stated Amelie.

"My dear, I would not have missed it. I am always out and about. I am just trying to shake this dreadful cold," he reasoned.

"I know. It will all get better soon, I know," she reassured him.

He looked appreciative; however, he remembered when it was he who would encourage her. The tables seemed to be turning as they often do. She was strong-spirited and knew that whatever the outcome, she would be there for her family.

"Yes, Uncle, they will get to the bottom of it," added Lars.

"That is right," replied Jenny as she clutched onto Hannah, who was on her lap. At this point she was still optimistic and knew that she would be strong for the family. She released Hannah and let the children play in the garden. They ran about until the early evening, when guests started to leave and they were the only ones left.

Jenny and Amelie insisted on clearing up whatever they could after the caterers. The family retired inside for digestifs before leaving. They remained hopeful that the summer would pan out as intended. The afternoon had brought back memories for Amelie and Hank of their childhood days and summers with Margaux—fond memories of bygone days still etched in the back of their memories.

A few days later Amelie called her aunt to express her gratitude and to mention how much she had enjoyed of the party.

"It was all so well planned, and I was so pleased to see everyone again," she related to Marguerite.

"Thank you. We so enjoyed having you again. And now a bit of bad news. Your uncle had a biopsy as they found a lump in his kidney. He is not well. You must prepare yourself. The doctors are doing all they can."

"Oh no. I am so sorry. I didn't think that it would be that serious. Will he be all right?"

"I do not know. They are hopeful, but we know how life can be. Look at what happened to your mother."

"I do not know what to say. I am beside myself with worry. Is there anything that I can do?"

"It is all under control. I did not want you to worry. He will be fine. He is resting as they have given him some treatment and he will undergo an operation. I do not know what to do. I am so used to having everything in order, but this I cannot control," she admitted despondently.

"If you need me, I am here for you all," Amelie promised.

"Thank you. If we need you, that will be perfect," Marguerite said obligingly, knowing that there was a long road ahead. "Unfortunately, we have put a hold on the summer plans. I suggest that you prepare to see your grandparents. We will have to get back to you regarding the end of summer in France. We are not certain where we will be then."

"OK. That is fine. We can put that off until we know the prognosis. I feel so down," Amelie admitted. She was so used to her aunt being her Rock of Gibraltar, but now that the situation was in reverse, she quickly had to step into her role and be the dedicated and supportive niece. It hadn't been that long ago when Marguerite took on the role of a dedicated and supportive aunt.

"Luckily it is in the early stages, so we can be optimistic. I had no idea and did not see any of this coming. He just started to feel bad. He had a chill at the party, and we went in straight after that. He has four weeks of treatment and then the operation to get the tumour out. And then more treatment, and then an assessment. Therefore, we will be here in the country and in London for the next three months until the end of the summer," Marguerite explained.

"Well, we are here and in the country. Lars gets back, and then we have the horse trials and the beginning of the season. So we can see him when he comes to hospital. We will pray for the best. I will let Dad know. Does Hank know?"

"No, not yet. I will tell him."

"Fine. Please get back to me with anything," Amelie offered.

"OK. Bye, dear. All our love to you."

"Thank you, and the same to you." Amelie disconnected despondently. It was beginning to look like an uncertain summer when it had all been planned so well. She thought of the previous summer. It was ideal as she was a newlywed. That summer was one enjoyable phase of one event after another. In May she was so optimistic about a new life and her business. Now reality had set in, and the euphoria was beginning to end.

She needed to speak with Lars, so she picked up the phone to ring him. He was her constant as Uncle Lance had been to her aunt. Their relationship was an example which she aspired to replicate. The two men seemed so similar, which had helped to continue the relationship. He was supportive of everything, including her close connection with her family.

"When are you coming home?"

"Tomorrow. We have wrapped up work here. I shall be on the first flight out," he promised.

"I cannot wait. I have just spoken to Auntie, and it is not good news. Lance is not well. It is a tumour in his kidney."

"So sorry to hear that, dear. How far along is he?"

"She says that there is hope and that he is in the initial stages. He needs to go in, and then he will be having treatment here all summer. I cannot believe it. It changes so much."

"I know. At least he will be close so we can see him and look after him," he consoled her.

"At least. Well, next on the calendar is the horse trials. Remember, we go to the country next weekend. Well, if he pulls through the operation OK," she reasoned.

"Look. We will plan it as it goes. One day at a time. If we are not up to it and you want to stay in London to keep an eye on things, that is completely fine."

"Splendid. You are so understanding. I need to be at the hospital with Marguerite. We really need to see her through this."

"We really do. Now try to keep your mind on your new client and expanding your business. He would be devastated to know that this is affecting you in any way."

"All right, dear. I will. Cheerio. And see you soon."

"See you tomorrow. I'll FaceTime you later," he assured her.

She knew that talking to him would do the trick. She felt more confident and at ease. She was uneasy and tried not to think of anything happening to Lars. How was her aunt managing?

Hank hung up with Jenny. Lance had been such a staying power in his life for years. He was the uncle who took him riding and footballing. He remembered the afternoons watching cricket at the club and fishing at the private pond. A whole lifetime of memories of holidays in England and France passed through his mind. It also resurfaced those memories of Margaux and how quickly her life was taken. That experience now became a precursor to prepare him for this unknown. He assured himself that the odds were in his favour and that medicine was much more advanced than a decade ago. He needed to call his uncle, but needed to map out what to say so as to not make him anxious. He decided to keep things on the surface and be cheerful because anything more would crush Lance. It was an anomaly that the weather was so perfect at such a daunting time.

If that were not enough to think about, the case had been advancing and the authorities were on the trail of the ringleader. It was all confidential; however, it coincided with the soon to be released men who were already serving their sentence. Hank and Nick were already up to date and had spoken to Roger, who had issued restraining orders against the perpetrators. They still had a few more weeks of safety; however, no one knew if something else would occur.

Chapter 3

Déjà Vu

A crisp end of May morning lured Amelie out of bed from a deep slumber. Lars had left for Malta, and she had had a rough week at work. Mr Mitchvale had a tour of London and Japan planned, and she wanted it all to be prefect for him. She opened her iPad and went over his travel details one final time.

The phone rang. "Hello. It's your father. Have I caught you at a bad time?"

It sounded serious. "No, Father, this is fine. Is something wrong?"

"Yes, apparently so. I am afraid that the culprits have been released early. There has been another attempt on another estate very similar to what happened here. We need to be more cautious. Now Lars became aware last night in Malta, and Roger is working on sorting out a restraining order. Just thought that you might like to know that the ringleader is still out there."

"How horrible! Shall we tell Auntie? She has so much on her mind," Amelie responded.

"Surely she should know. I suppose that Hank will contact her. I do not want you worked up. It is all behind us."

Amelie had memories of just before she'd gotten married and of the New Year's Eve celebration on the island, and then of receiving a call from her aunt in France about the issues. It was such a damper on the event. Since then her life had been so optimistic and cheerful. It was as if someone had unearthed the bad memories and her mother's privacy along with them. It would be even worse for her aunt, who was concentrating on her husband, Lance. Amelie needed Lars back home and now.

She knew that the day would come when the perpetrators would be freed, and it seemed to have crept up sooner, to her immense disappointment. She was alone in the flat and waited until the housekeeper arrived. Lars was not due until the next day, and then there was the gala, followed by a weekend in the country watching the horse show with Lars and her country retriever, Ginny. Hank, Jenny, and the children would be joining them for a picnic on the lawns. If she could just think of the happy days, then everything should be fine.

She had a sense of security in the flat as she had been there since she was a child and was bequeathed it by her mother. The voices of guests and loved ones still echoed against the walls. She peered out of the bay window onto the familiar scene of her back garden with periwinkles, bluebells, and assorted tulips and azaleas.

The phone rang again. It was Lars.

"Dear, I am just checking to see if you are OK. No doubt you have spoken to Nick by now. I am so sorry, dear. I will be home tomorrow, and all will be fine," he reassured her.

"Thank you for that. I was hoping that you would call. I am so happy to hear from you. What time will you be back?" she asked eagerly.

"By lunchtime. I am taking an earlier flight. Managed to wrap things up until next time. It is never-ending. I miss you and will be home soon. I promise."

"Lovely, dear. I cannot wait to see you. It is all a bit horrifying, and I want you here."

"I will be there in two shakes. See you soon. And call me later," he replied obligingly.

Not feeling much better, she stayed in, working on her iPad, until Marietta arrived. She worked from home on her new clients' accounts until ringing her brother to see what could be done about Lance.

"Well, I think that we should wait for the prognosis. He is getting the best care here, and he can now devote the summer to recuperating," he advised.

"I know, but I feel so useless. At least we can visit him in hospital," she reassured.

"Yes, but we would not want to contaminate him. He could run the risk of infection. Be there for Auntie, and we can see him later at home."

"Sounds good. You always know how to put things into perspective. Thanks again. I'll see you all soon. We have to talk about that other thing, remember?"

"How could I forget? It is all so gruelling. When will it ever end?"

"Who knows?" she stated. They disconnected. She would spend another Friday evening waiting for Lars and watching Netflix. It was becoming mundane, and she wished that she could ban all business trips for the next year.

Nicholas and Nadia had planned a night at the theatre. The West End was buzzing. The bright lights and billboards embodied the entertainment culture as they waited on line to present their tickets for the show. Nadia, excited about the notion, had dressed to the nines and was looking forward to the post theatre dinner near Drury Lane. For Nicholas, it was different from his usual Mayfair club, but Nadia wanted an evening out among the stage stars. They took their seats and romantically huddled in their booth until the curtains rose. Nadia had requested a musical full of emotion and symphony to enlighten her creative cravings. Dreaming of being on the stage, she glanced at Nick, who was not the slightest bit aware of her ambitions. She was only in her thirties and could still rekindle an old dream. She could shed the routine lifestyle of the committed wife, set herself with for a life of theatre and drama, and have eventful evenings with friends on the West End. She imagined herself dressed glamorously every evening.

Nadia's background was filled with dressing up and being on show. She too was from a retail background and had spent her early years studying drama and seeing shows with friends. She was a fashionista who had ballet and dance lessons. She craved that lifestyle once more. She was tiring of the lunches and regattas.

She found herself harmoniously following each stanza and tapping her feet with the tune. She had decided to take classes again and had no idea how to tell Nick. Summer in London would be the perfect time to do it, and then he could come and watch her perform. With the final curtain call, she felt herself yearning for more. They applauded with a standing ovation, and he gently guided her out of the booth and to the waiting car to take them to dinner.

"Hungry, darling?" he asked.

"Famished, dear," she replied.

"Did you enjoy the performance?"

"Absolutely. I think I want to start again, dear," she confessed.

"Oh, we will see about that," he responded nonchalantly.

"Yes," she replied. She knew full well that she would do it and just needed the opportune time to tell him.

For Amelie, Saturday morning could not come soon enough. She had a meal in and had an early night. She had received Lars's text that he was on his way. She had the brunch prepared as usual. He would expect the usual, although he would have eaten in the lounge and then on the plane in club class.

She clambered downstairs. The aroma of Marietta's brewing and coffee and eggs was circulating through the pantry. Amelie plopped on the settee and watched through the bay windows. Lars's car pulled up, and the chauffer assisted with the bags as he rummaged for the keys. She ran to the doorway and opened it for him.

"Hello, darling," she greeted.

"Hello, dear." He embraced her after a long trip.

"So good to see you finally. I feel like it has been ages."

"No. Not so long, not so long. Let me get my bags in. Well, something does smell nice."

"We have made the usual. Hungry?" she asked mischievously.

"Famished," he responded.

"That's a relief," she replied.

Lars devoured the meal as if it were his first of the day.

"Thank you, dear.

"Thank you, Marietta," he called out to the kitchen, where she was clearing up.

"You are welcome, Mr Faverer. I am happy that you enjoyed it," she replied. She was pleased that she had accomplished another successful brunch and was planning the next duty.

Lars and Amelie relaxed on the settee, where they laughed, chatted and flicked through the channels and the magazines on their tablets. He provided a calming environment wherein she was assured of his support. It would be a long and difficult summer, unlike the one that she had imagined.

"What do you say that after the trials and the operation and the regatta, we go to your grandparents'? I have some time off in a few weeks. It would be just what you need. Sailing, Winifred, and Lionel."

"Really? Superb. It would be just what I need to spend some time away. Lance will be convalescing, and Marietta can look after the house. Dad will be travelling. I will only miss Hank and Jenny," she reasoned.

"I suppose they can come too. I think that someone should be here in case something happens," he suggested.

"I suppose," she said despondently.

"Let's go out for dinner. We can go to Delilah's again. It is your favourite."

"OK. Delilah's it is." Only the crème brûlée and the braised duck could comfort her.

The afternoon wore on, and they sipped tea on the balcony before preparing to go out.

"Thanks for the me time," she said.

"Not a problem. You would do it for me, I am sure."

"Yes. I think so." She realised how selfish she was being and asked about his parents, Dixon and Alice.

"They are splendid. No issues ever, thankfully."

It was one of the reasons that she loved him. His life was so drama-free and regular, unlike hers, which had an issue every month which revived in the crevices. If only her life were simple. It struck a balance of being privileged having its hindrances.

"That's good."

"I'll start planning the trip tomorrow. Leave it up to me," he offered.

It was a quiet afternoon for Nadia, who was still euphoric from the evening before. The show had inspired her. She was to spend the Mayfair afternoon practising her lines and exercising her voice for Monday night's class. She had told Nick that she was going to an arts festival event, when in fact she would be in her leggings and sweats honing her talent. She wanted to surprise him. She had many old monologues to go through. She had files on tape and practised new ones. She went over them again and again until she had them all memorised, with new songs to add to her portfolio.

Her files included plays by Shakespeare, Pinter, Chekhov, Stanislavski, Bergman, and Coward, all from her early days at the theatre. She had given it up to have a solid job to take care of her parents, and then she met Nicholas, who married her. She now had the confidence to return. She had been stifled these past few years. She had been living in the shadow of Margaux and her life. Nadia had tried to be the best wife Nicholas had known, but it was time to spread her own wings. She had waited for the wedding to pass, and then the news about the case had resurfaced, so it never seemed like a good time. She was going to network to get back into form.

She imagined that she was onstage with her voice projected to the back of the room. She drew breaths to get through the lines and spoke as she released. She went from the top and repeated herself over and over until she had reached perfection. She looked at her watch. Nicholas would soon be back from lunch at the club.

Marguerite packed a small overnight bag to take with her to the operating theatre. She also had helped Lance gather what he needed and hoped that he would be released in a week's time. The car would pick them up bright and early and take them to London, where he would be admitted. He was meant to be in theatre by noon and then out by four. She dreaded how she would get through those hours while he was in operation. She looked forward to being with her family.

Marguerite enjoyed the golden moments with Lance that Saturday. She did not know what the outcome would be and prayed for the best. In front of him she was strong and wanted to see him through. Friends had been calling to wish him the best, and he was almost relishing the attention. Lance was optimistic and wanted to see them all once he had recovered.

By Wednesday Marguerite was a nervous wreck. They arrived at the pre-theatre facility early that morning to prepare him for surgery. He had been meticulous with his diet the following days and with his pre-surgery preparations. Marguerite watched as Lance was readied by the nurses. The doctors arrived for a brief consultation, followed by the anaesthesiologist, who was the last person she saw before leaving for the waiting area. Marguerite kissed her husband tenderly on the forehead and whispered, "I love you and will see you later." She was careful not to show any emotion. If it was the last time she were to see him, she wanted him to remember her as she was and not to have any fear.

It was already 9.30 a.m. Amelie had taken the morning off to sit with her aunt. When she arrived, Marguerite was stoic yet frazzled. She sat poised and raised her head from her magazine as Amelie approached.

"Hello, darling. He has just gone in," she informed her.

"I see. How was he?"

"He was fine. Still optimistic and relaxed."

"That is a relief. How are you?"

"Fine," she answered, subdued. "I hate hospitals. It is probably why I never had any children. I do not know how to handle this new routine."

"It will be fine," Amelie reassured her aunt. "I'm here. Would you like me to get you something? Coffee? Tea? A croissant?"

"Sure, that would be great. I have not had anything as Lance could not eat this morning."

"OK. I will get you something."

"Amelie, thank you for coming. It means a lot to us to have you here. He is resting assured that I am not alone. I have not been to a hospital in this capacity since Margaux. What a trial and tribulation that was. However, she left behind such a beautiful gift. Her children were all she cherished in the world. How selfish I have been not to have told her that enough."

"Oh, thank you. Do not worry. This will all work out, you'll see. I am sure that Mummy knew how you really felt. You were always together. When we were children, we knew it. Don't preoccupy yourself with this. Lance will be fine. And then we will have that summer that we wanted."

"I know. You are right," she replied sceptically.

"I'll just get up and get the tea, and then I'll be right back." Amelie got up and walked away, mostly to pull herself together in front of her aunt. It would be useless if she were a bundle of emotions. However, it did bring back the feeling that she had dreaded for years. It was an unexpected rush of memory that almost paralysed her. She could barely think. She picked up the phone to call Hank.

He answered straightaway. "Hello. Any news?"

"No. Uncle Lance is in surgery and should be out by one."

"I see. How is Auntie doing?"

"She's as good as she can be. She started talking about Mummy. I don't know, I suppose."

"I see. Sounds a bit unsettling," he confided in her.

"Yes. I think so. She'll be OK though. As soon as he gets the all-clear."

"I know. Keep me posted. I will pop in this evening to see him after work."

"OK. I shall be gone by then. I'll be back in the office by this afternoon. I'll stay until after lunch."

"Splendid. Cheerio."

"Bye."

Amelie pulled herself together and returned with the tea and croissant. She handed them to her aunt cautiously and then sat next to her and waited. They waited for hours and chatted about holidays and anything that Amelie could think of to take her aunt's mind off the reality of the situation. The time spent was gruelling as she nervously looked towards the surgery area to see if someone would come out. Eventually, the attendant approached.

"Mrs Morris, your husband is out of surgery and is resting in the recovery area. You will be able to see him soon. Then doctor will see you then."

"Thank you," Marguerite replied, relieved.

"Great," responded Amelie, relieved. She looked at her aunt and nodded. "The worst is over."

"Yes, he has made it through. Now for the tricky part: the recovery."

"It'll all be fine. I will wait a little longer and then get back to work. Would you like anything?"

"No thank you. I am fine. I will wait to hear what has happened," she responded nervously.

"All right. Give Uncle my love. I will call him when he is more awake."

"Sure. All my love, dear. And thank you," she replied.

"Right. I will get going. Talk to you both soon. Hank will be here in a few hours."

"Bye, dear."

"Bye."

Amelie was relieved when she walked away. It was in the early stages, and nothing had gone horribly wrong. She pictured her uncle lying there and wanted to see him lively again. Seeing him in this state would be too much to take. She messaged Hank the news and walked out of the hospital.

She called Lars to update him from the office. He was relieved and planned to visit; however, he wanted to plan the holiday for Amelie as she had been through so much. The firm had gotten the news that Shadrock and Mesnel would be out in a few weeks, and he wanted her far away.

"How is he doing?"

"I did not see him; Hank is going later. Perhaps we can see him later."

"I see. I will contact your aunt when this is all over to show my concern."

"That would be a good idea."

"Are you ready to leave in two weeks?"

"I think that would be perfect. Just in time to see Lance through and then get away."

"Fine then. It is all sorted. Do you want to stay at the resort?"

"I think that would be best so as to not overburden Nan."

"Right then. Will do. If there is nothing else, dear, I must be pressing on with work."

"Sure. See you later."

"Bye. See you later."

Her conversations were always so short. She was the type who wanted to elaborate on the phone, but Lars never had the time. She directed her concentration towards Mr Mitchvale and his many travels. She was planning his trip to the United States and had all her connections in New York at bay.

Marguerite held Lance's hand as he awoke from the surgery. His eyes widened to ensure that he was in the room with her. She smiled as he smiled back, knowing that he was done.

"You are fine, dear. It all went well. How do you feel?"

He nodded and mumbled something.

"That's good. You made it. The surgeon will be back, and Hank will be here later."

"I am a bit sore here," he said as he pointed to his abdomen.

"I know. I think that it is normal. They will give you some more painkillers, I think."

She said whatever she could to relieve him. "They have removed it all. Thank heavens."

"Good," he muttered.

"Do you need more rest?"

"I think so. I am a bit drowsy."

"I know. Get your rest. I will be here." He nodded off for a short while and came to later. By that evening, Hank had arrived.

"Auntie, Uncle, how are you?"

"Fine, dear. I see that you got access all right."

"Yes. Not a problem. Almost walked through."

"Uncle, how are you feeling?"

Lance nodded in reply.

"I can only stay a few moments. I hope that you can manage. Will you spend the evening here?"

"I think I had better. I do not want to leave him until he is stronger."

"I think that is best. If you need anything, just let me know. Jenny and I have plans later, but just ring me." He stayed and chatted for a few more minutes. "Shall I get you anything before I leave?"

"Yes. Some tea, dear. If it is not too much trouble."

"Sure, I can. No trouble at all." He left diligently to find the beverage machine and returned quickly. He smiled as he handed his aunt the cup. "I am relieved that it went well. You say that they have removed the tumour?"

"Yes. Thankfully. There is still chemo and now physio."

"Good news. That is a relief," he replied, looking over at Lance, concerned.

"So lovely to see you again. Send my best to Jenny and the children."

"I will. Take care, Uncle, and take care of yourself, Auntie. I will speak to you soon."

Marguerite was relieved that she had such a wonderful nephew who was so concerned about them both. She was right: Margaux had done so many things right. Hank had his father's walk, which was so stately and pronounced. *He should have gone into the foreign service instead of stocks and bonds,* she thought to herself. She was able to overlook his nouveaux tendencies because he was so loyal. She watched him leave and then turned to Lance and gripped his hand.

Hank composed himself at the exit and took out his phone to call home and then ring Amelie. He was a bit shattered by Lance's appearance. It showed his immortality and vulnerability and that life was always changing.

"He looks OK. It seems that he will recover fine," he remarked to Amelie.

"I know. Can't help but worry though," she admitted.

"Right. Just go and see him when he is better. Probably not tomorrow," he advised.

"I see. I really want to see them. Maybe Friday."

"That would be better. He still needs to recover."

"All right," she said despondently. "I will talk to you soon."

"Cheerio. Chat soon." He hung up.

It would be a hectic drive to his family home in the countryside in the rush hour traffic. He started the ignition and drove away.

Amelie basked in the glory, knowing that in twenty-four hours she would be at Winifred's. She went through her bags to ensure that she had everything for the two weeks. It seemed like a very long time. She would have to work amid the holiday environment. She was very used to that and had done it countless times.

Lars had scheduled everything. The trip was just in time to whisk her away from the villains who were being released from prison. She was still planning a trip to the Continent at the end of the summer and hoped that their releases would not ruin her plans. Furthermore, the ringleader had not been caught, and it was feared that he was still in close proximity. Kexan Shadrock and Tom Mesnel would not speak, and since the case was over and they had spent their time, they were not obligated to say anything unless they were subpoenaed or new evidence had arisen, it seemed. The family would not want to pursue them and have it all dragged out from beneath the woodwork again. Thirty million euros of Renaissance art had appreciated in value and was now worth forty-five million. It was at a foundation museum in Marseille, safely guarded. It was impossible that it would be the target of another attempted heist. Also, with new technology, it would be difficult for someone to assume Amelie's mother's identity. The previous attempt was hopefully a one-off chance. She and Lars had been careless. As Lars had suggested, their whole system had been revamped to prevent this type of thing from happening again.

Amelie was reassured and optimistic about the summer again. Lance was out of the woods and recovering, Nicholas and Hank were content, and she and Lars were planning a future.

The car arrived to pick them up routinely. She had been taking this route since childhood, and it had become more like a commute for her. It was early and by 2 p.m. Eastern time they were meant to have landed and be miles away from everything. The car pulled up to the airport, where they disembarked and headed to the kiosk. Lars had secured business-class seats, but that was irrelevant. Amelie was just concerned about a lovely early summer day on the island. She could imagine the blooming branches hanging along the route they drove to Nan's house. She would not have it any other way and insisted on their staying in the guest house. Amelie breathed in as she imagined the orange-red sky at sunset and the smell of the salt water from the sea to the villa. There were fond memories as just yards away she and Lars had been married. It had been almost three years already. It was such a comfortable and cosy environment of which she had nostalgic memories since childhood.

The departure lounge was abuzz as they waited for their flight. Lars bumped into a few business colleagues who were heading out for the summer. He and Amelie had planned a trip for two weeks, but it was enough considering the issues they were leaving behind. Amelie had high hopes for her uncle, who was recuperating well with chemo. Her father would hold down the fort until she returned, and Hank was monitoring the case. It was all under control. She was relieved.

Amelie and Lars boarded the plane on time and had a very smooth flight to Bermuda. She enjoyed the in-flight entertainment and the hundreds of channels. Lars read the whole flight, showing himself to be the workaholic that he was. They disembarked hastily and headed to the arrivals area. There was a car waiting for them as her grandfather was now too unsteady to drive. They had a smooth drive to the house.

The home could be seen from the top of the driveway as it stood on the hill with the veranda winding around it. There were blossoming bougainvillea and poincianas, as well as daffodils. Winifred also loved roses. The staff were quickly preparing for their arrival under Winnie's orders. The car stopped, and Simon arrived to assist with the baggage. Lionel heard the car arrive and called for Winnie, who was preparing in the back. She quickly came out to the sitting room near the door and called for Verena to come out of the kitchen.

"Verena, they are here. Lionel has gone to see them. You can get the table ready for tea." They had prepared boiled fish and johnnycake— something light because it was late in London and her guests would have had something on the plane. Winnie knew the routine and had been lucky enough to welcome Amelie and Lars countless times.

"Simon, Grandpapa, how are you all?" she greeted her family.

"Wonderful. Finally arrived after a long flight again. Lovely to be here," she replied as she heard the waves echoing in the background.

"Lionel, Simon, hello," greeted Lars.

"Hello, Lars. Had a good flight?" asked Lionel.

"Yes, it was perfect as usual."

"Good, let me help you. Anything else?" asked Lionel as he looked around for more bags.

"Here, can you take this one, please?" Amelie offered her bag.

"Sure." The group walked in to see Winne sitting on the wicker sofa waiting for them.

Amelie rushed towards her as she had when she was younger and hugged and kissed her.

"How have you been, my lovely?" asked Winifred.

"Fine now, Grandmama. It is all good now." Amelie had arrived at her refuge. It was her home away from home. "It all smells so good," she confided. "Where's Verena?"

"She just dashed in the kitchen. We know that you all must be ravenous."

"Grandma Winnie, how are you?" asked Lars. "Lovely to see you. And thank you for your hospitality. Amelie is over the moon."

"Not to worry. I am fine, dear. It is always a pleasure to have my granddaughter. Now the meal is waiting for you as soon as you sort yourselves in the guest house. Verena has been working all afternoon to get it right for you."

"Thank you. We will be right back out," promised Lars. The couple gathered their things, and Simon assisted them to the guest house. It was a cosy two-bedroom cottage with a separate entrance and patio. The walked down the winding path on the back lawn and to the front door. The entrance was filled with vases of flowers, and food items stocked in the fridge.

"My, it is lovely. She should not have gone through so much trouble," commented Amelie as she looked around the quaint kitchen.

"I know. It's great." Lars was excited as he saw most of his favourite home-made snacks already in the fridge, along with a lovely Moët & Chandon. "Look! They really should not have," he stated delighted as he opened the fridge. "Dessert." Lars was pleased to see a large island rum cake covered with walnuts. There was also a box of truffles and a starter selection of snacks in case they wanted a late morning.

"That is so thoughtful," Amelie observed as she watched him. "They have thought of everything. Look, everything is so fresh," she noted as she picked up some tropical fruit. The guavas and mangoes were ripe. Winifred had several major mango trees in her garden. Some were more southern, which Amelie loved.

"I know," admitted Lars as he bit into a sweet apple on the counter. He enjoyed the freedom of the little cottage, which had an entrance leading to the brisk ocean. It was not a day for surfing; however, he knew that they would have a few days out on the boat during the trip. Nicholas was a skilled boater with a Boston whaler that Amelie cherished for the fond memories of years on the water with her family. The family was a smaller one, but she'd enjoyed helping her parents pack the basket of goods to carry on the boat. She enjoyed the tortillas, salsa, and guacamole as well as other baked French treats from her mother, Margaux. She recalled that Winifred was not a big boater. Her grandmother spent the weekends at the boutique or travelling to buy merchandise to sell. She also spent time in the garden fully clothed in linen and wearing a wide-brimmed straw hat. From the French doors Amelie could see her flowers bloom and swaying in the sea wind. There were bougainvillea and azaleas as well as the hibiscus. Amelie could still remember their sweet sap that she would taste when smaller.

"Are you hungry, dear? Perhaps we should unpack later and get over to the main house," Lars suggested.

"Certainly. Grandmama is waiting, and we do not really want to be a burden. I do feel as though she expects us to do our own thing."

"Yes. Shall we head over then?"

"Sure. You lead the way," she joked. She knew that she was much more accustomed to the house. However, they had been together a long time.

Winifred and Lionel were waiting while Verena prepared the table with the food. It was a light meal as she knew that it was late for Lars and Amelie now and almost 9 p.m. in London.

"There you are, dears. Is the cottage all right?" asked Winifred

"It is fantastic. Thank you for the lovely cake, fruit, truffles, and champagne. Also, the goodies in the fridge. We hope that we have not put you out too much," responded Amelie.

"Not at all. It was my pleasure, dear, and I am glad that you like it all. Verena made the cake. It was my mother's recipe. And Lionel found the truffles in town. The lovely fruit is from the garden and the market. Let me know if either of you needs anything else. We would be happy to get it for you while you are here."

"Thank you so much," replied Lars, who was used to her contributions.

"Yes. Really. We have two weeks this time, and it will be

splendid," assured Amelie as she sat at the table. "Oh, Verena, it all smells delicious." She relished the scent of the bay leaves and the baking cake.

"I know you love this dish," reminded Verena.

"I certainly do." They all sat at the table and started to serve the broth and the cakes to one another. Something else was brewing in the kitchen with a very sweet and spicy aroma. It must have been some sort of raisin and carrot spice cake with cream cheese icing, something Amelie remembered from her days as a little girl.

"Do you know when Nicholas will be down?" asked Winifred.

"I think later in the summer. They are so enjoying all the events, and he has the regatta lined up. I have the horse trials. We should be back for the end of Wimbledon," informed Amelie.

"I see. Have you heard that Nadia is working towards a production in the West End?" asked Winifred.

"Really? No. I had not heard. However, she has been a bit busy recently. I suppose that it is the reason."

"Yes. I was a bit surprised that she is going back to the theatre."

"I know. However, she does seem to have a lot of time on her hands. I am so happy that she has been able to do something. I mean, she would not have wanted an office job again, and this is her talent, right?" reasoned Amelie.

"I suppose so," responded Winifred, undeterred. Simon and Lars tucked in, unaware of the news.

Amelie and Winifred caught up on Lance's progress and the dreaded case that was looming and threatening her happiness. It was like releasing a burden once she spoke to Winifred about it all. Lars was able to reassure her and advised that they retire as maybe the long day was making her a bit overwrought.

"We will try to think of that another time, when you have had some rest, dear."

"I know. It is just that in a few weeks we could have an ordeal again," she responded.

"Not to worry. It is all under control. They are not able to return, and there should be no problems in France. They are close to finding the ringleader of the gang, and then it will all be over. Perhaps they ensured their freedom by assisting with the investigation. We will never know. They may no longer be a threat," assured Lars.

"You are such a wonderful young man," commented Winifred.

"Yes, he is right, Amelie. They are no longer a concern, and you are safe here in this island paradise with us. We have the best security and cameras and alarms. We can hire an extra guard for your safety if you wish," offered Lionel.

"Thanks, Grandpapa, but that will not be necessary. I am all right here, and I do feel safe and sound. There are still so many unanswered questions, such as how they had managed to steal Mummy's documents and how they knew to target us. It perturbs me. How did they know my movements and that the documents were in the box? I mean, they must have been watching for a very long time. I never noticed anyone, and I have been on that street for such a long time now. It is one of the reasons that I feel safer at the property of the luxury firm rather than running about on the streets every day."

"We know. And you have made the right choice. Not to worry about the unanswered. They were caught, and the authorities know the facts. Perhaps they had hacked into the surveillance system and did not have to worry about combing the streets, or perhaps they got into the high street bank's system. Whatever the issue, it cannot happen again. There have been safeguards put in place," assured Lars. The documents were now all in a private vault somewhere.

"That is good to know, dear. Grandmama and Grandpapa, I do think that it has been a very lovely and long day. I am always so happy to see you both. The meal was delicious as usual. And do not worry about us. We will have an early breakfast since we are both on London time, and then we will come over. Lars and I want to go out on the boat."

"Wonderful, dear. Do pop over for lunch or tea then. Have a lovely evening, and do not worry, Amelie," replied Winifred.

They left and walked over the cottage. Winifred looked at Lionel helplessly. "It is taking its toll worse than we thought, dear," she confided.

"I know. Just give her some time. We can only assure her of her safety and hope for the best."

"What more can we do? She is petrified from this ordeal still. She had a wedding and a new business, and still there has not been much progress."

"Perhaps Nicholas has an answer. Remember, she is worried about Lance," he observed.

"Perhaps it is that then. A day out on the boat should do her some good."

Amelie and Lars fell asleep as soon as their heads sank into their pillows. Amelie let her worries go and felt secure at her home away from home.

Chapter 4

Boating Days

Amelie and Lars arose when the day it was still dawning. The sun's rays were skimming the ocean's surface. They sat on the small patio, sipped their morning coffee, and glanced at their tablets before venturing over to wish the family and staff good morning. The Boston whaler was docked at the marina. It would take twenty minutes to get there.

"Perhaps I should pack the basket?"

"Sure, whatever you want. We do not leave until about nine. Would you like some sweet bread and avocado? There is a large mango on the counter," he offered.

"Sounds wonderful. We should save the mango for the basket. You know how I love to devour mangoes on the beach."

"Right you are." He smirked, having had many experiences with her on the shoreline when she was so systematic about her cravings and indulgences. It had been the right choice to visit when things were heating up back in London. He arose to gather the condiments and brought them to the breakfast table.

"It looks lovely, darling," Amelie observed affectionately, relishing anything from him. "Any news?" She was eager to find out if the case had advanced.

"Nothing, dear," Lars answered, when in fact there had been. The authorities were closing in on the ringleader, and news was imminent.

Winifred and Lionel awoke early, anticipating seeing their guests off to the marina. Verena had arrived at 7 a.m. to prepare the breakfast. She had switched her expertise to organic and healthy meals for the family. They had strict dietary requirements, and Amelie was also careful.

Winifred heard a knock on the French doors. Verena answered it.

"Morning, dears," she said.

"Morning, Verena. It all smells so lovely as usual. What have you made?"

"Egg white omelettes and wholegrain toast. There are some banana pancakes for Lars."

"Wonderful. I'll tuck right in."

"Amelie, how is the cottage, dear?" asked Winifred.

"Good morning, Grandmama. It's great. We watched the sunrise from the patio with some sweet bread and avocado."

"Lovely. Verena has prepared something here. I hope that you are still hungry."

"Famished, Winifred," answered Lars, looking forward to his favourite treat.

"Good. There is just enough time to have something before you head out. Have you a basket packed? Verena has a few things for you."

"That would be lovely. Thanks," Amelie responded obligingly.

"Verena, you can give her the treats for the day." Turning back to Amelie, she asked, "Will we see you later for tea or dinner?"

"We should be back by then. We will not go far, will we?" Amelie replied, turning to Lars.

"Not at all. Just along the shoreline," reassured Lars.

"All right. We will see you all later," replied Winifred.

It was exhilarating on the boat when the weather was calm. The plan was to encircle the island and view the towns from the ocean.

The boat was docked and ready. Between the two of them, they had enough skill to navigate through the water. They carried the basket and towels from the car and boarded. Amelie pulled the anchor while Lars steered out to the open water.

The water was calm, and the boat steadily glided through the water as it picked up speed. Amelie held on to the side as she stood near Lars. The breeze whisked through their hair as he accelerated and they encircled the island.

"Do you want to find a place to stop off?"

"Let's go to our special beach," he suggested.

"Yes. Let's!" she exclaimed. It was already 11 a.m. when they docked the boat and let down the anchor. The water was shallow. They carried a few jugs and some fruit with them to the shore. Lars took the items from Amelie as they waded to the shore and walked up the beach to a shady spot. There was a natural breeze, which would soon subside once the sun shone at high noon.

Amelie stretched out on the towel while Lars neared her, sipping his coconut water from the jug. They were worlds away from the hustle and bustle of the city of London.

"Would you ever want to live here permanently?" he asked.

"I love our home so much. We have the house and the flat and the horses. There is so much that is different. I feel as though this is an outpost and extension of my lifestyle there, but not the main part of my life. I suppose that it would be different if I had been raised here. I simply have not. There is Europe. Why do you ask?" she responded.

"No. It is just that people think that I should live here, and I was wondering how you feel."

"No. Do not listen to those people. They have no idea about your personal exposure and how different life can be. Grandmama had to travel just to shop for her boutique. It is not that easy to make a living. We have to be practical. It is good for so many things but just not everything like what we are used to."

"I see. I'm just asking." He did not want to push it further.

She smiled and gazed at the sky. "Wouldn't it be nice to have hardly anything to worry about all day? But we do have so much to contend with. Like the case and Uncle Lance."

"I know. It seems like that was all ages ago, and we have only been here a day."

"It is what life is like here. It feels so far away."

"I am not sure that I want to be away from everything all the time."

They talked and laughed some more. It was almost three. They had promised Winifred that they would be back for tea, and they wanted to miss the rush hour traffic from the marina.

"Let's head back. Nan is waiting," Amelie suggested.

"Let's," he said, unenthused.

They were quiet on the return as the sun had dipped past its high noon position. It was still sweltering, and the cool sea breeze refreshed their systems.

Winnie had an assortment of cakes and treats laid out for tea. She and Lionel sat on the veranda, sipping an afternoon aperitif, until Lars and Amelie arrived. The bougainvillea and vines hung on the latticework to provide more shade as the blossoms caught the breeze from the ocean whisking towards their home.

"They should be back soon," commented Winnie.

"Yes. It is a perfect afternoon, and the weather is brilliant," he agreed.

"The lazy, hazy days of summer."

"That's right. And may we continue to see many more."

They heard the engine of the Range Rover approach. Amelie disembarked, deeper in tone than she'd been that morning. She had not seen herself in the mirror and was eager to assess the results of the day out on her skin.

"Hello, Grandmama, Grandpapa," she greeted them as they approached.

"Hello, dears. How did it go? Well, you look sun kissed," observed Winnie.

"Oh, do not worry. I wore sunscreen, and we sat in the shade," Amelie assured her.

"It was glorious. Just what we needed after the hustle and bustle of the city," agreed Lars.

"Well, good. Would you like a quick drink before tea? Come and join us," offered Lionel.

"Absolutely, Leo. In a sec. I just want to freshen up," replied Lars.

"Yes, we will be right back. I just want to wash a bit of the salt off," explained Amelie.

"Fabulous, dears. See you in a bit," stated Winne.

Lars was eager to check his emails as it was night-time in London and he'd had no reception on the boat. He was expecting Roger to update him on the case. They wandered to the cottage. Amelie rushed to the shower while he got his technology together. He read the email, and the news was not as expected. The restraining order had been revoked, and still there were no updates on the ringleader. The gang were not being cooperative.

Amelie returned, refreshed and dressed in a summer linen dress.

"You look splendid," he commented.

"Thank you, dear. Are you ready? Nan and Grandpapa are expecting us." They wandered back to the front of the house through the side garden and sat and enjoyed the hilltop view of the ocean.

"This is just what I needed. It is so different from the city. Will you ever come for a visit?" asked Amelie.

"No, dear. We have had our time. We have lovely memories and souvenirs, and that will have to suffice."

"Such a shame. Sometimes we miss you all so much over there," added Amelie.

"You are always welcome here," responded Lionel.

"How about some tea? The cakes have been out for a while."

Lars and Lionel followed Amelie to the table. Lars was still disturbed by the news. He thought that maybe they should extend their trip. He knew that Amelie would be deflated as the summer balls were under way.

The couple passed the afternoon with Winifred and Lionel in the spacious living room that brought back fond memories. Amelie could hear the echoes of laughter of the bygone years and see the images of guests and her parents who had been in its presence. This familiarity brought a form of comfort to her. She had been visiting the house since she could remember. The garden was vast. She and Hank would rummage through the tropical vegetation. It was a breezy evening. She shuddered as she tightened her shawl across her shoulders.

It had been a foggy day in London. The dry air had brought poor visibility as well as uncertainty. Hank and Roger were despondent over the news. Nicholas was concerned and wanted to straighten things out before Amelie's return. He still felt as though she could be in danger and that her safety was key. Regardless, the best thing to do would be to tell her so that she could take the necessary precautions—sooner rather than later.

"I cannot believe that they have not given us more to go on," Nicholas stated to Hank.

"I know. We have been left guessing as to whether they cracked the case from the beginning. We will never be able to ascertain if they got everyone. Apparently they have not."

"That is the problem with the gangs. There will always be more involved than you know."

"I suppose that the police just want to be certain and are very close," suggested Nicholas.

"Let us hope so. This could happen again," warned Hank.

"I am not so certain. We have more precautions in place."

"Criminals are getting better. You have read about the hackers. It would have been worse had this been computer documents rather than hard copies. Digitisation brings the risk of uncertainty," advised Hank.

"Be that as it may, we must still listen to the professionals on this. Shadrock and Mesnel must talk. They are out and can speak."

"What if they are in danger and cannot talk? Which is probably why they want to be in the UK rather than over there. Obviously, they are running too."

"Obviously that is just what it is. In the meantime, what are we to do? Amelie returns in a week, and then she will be in all the social columns with her events. She will be a moving target this summer. Perhaps we can negotiate with them ourselves," suggested Nicholas.

"I do not know. The authorities have warned against that. It might make matters worse. It may be deeper than we thought. There might be a different motive for what has happened. What if they did not just want the money? What if it was deeper? But what could it be?"

"I think that we are overthinking. Everyone has a price. This lot surely do."

"It would be in the millions to negotiate with them," advised Hank.

"What if they are expecting that? They must realise that their release ups the stakes for Amelie."

"Someone wants the paintings and will pay a price to get them. They still are not secure. It must be an art broker. It has to be a circle of crime. But who?"

"What if it is an old client or someone you have come across? It will be only a matter of time before they get to Amelie again. Especially since she is in the industry that she is in now. We should check to see if there are any new clients," advised Nicholas.

"Surely they will not try that again. It may be how they got to her the first time. All of those appointments all over London."

"That is why they need a smokescreen. Someone we trust. But who?"

"Well, the answer might be in a listing that we have and over-looked. We have been taken for a ride all along."

"I think so, Dad. I certainly think so," Hank agreed.

"That is it. First thing in the morning we shall get on this. There must be a history with someone with a personal grievance or even a contender of the assets back in France. After a number of years, per-haps there were challenges. We will have to look at your grandfather's business dealings. There was a time when he was meant to have sold them, but that deal turned sour. We will see."

"Right you are. We will get on it straightaway."

Nicholas poured some bourbon from the bar. Nadia had another evening out and would not be back until ten. He sighed, uncertain of how long it would take and whether she would make it as an actress again. Her looks had matured since her earlier days. What made her think that this would all work out again? *Forty is the new twenty,* he thought. He got to work and searched some old files down in the den. He came across a photo of Margaux. It was one that she'd had done by a photographer off the Kings Road. The children were still young, as was she. He wanted to keep her legacy clean and not have her gifts ruined in name. Everything about her was so sincere and genuine; she did not deserve this dragging through the mud. Her turquoise eyes still pierced, even from the grave. He went into some files from the 1960s and thought why he had kept them. It all should have been stored or digitised. He looked through names and came across one in particular, Guillaume Deneuve. The family ties were strained since Louis had decided not to place the paintings in his gallery. It was years ago, and back then they were valued at half the price, not their value of forty-five million euros today. Deneuve was a diplomatic colleague who also had a line of French aristocratic links in his family and collected art. He could not still be alive. Maybe he had issue who had gotten involved with someone. Nicholas never thought to go to the authorities before as it had never had crossed his mind.

The initial search concluded that although Deneuve had passed in 1992, there was still issue who were in their sixties. Could it be that someone still desired the paintings or thought that the family had some right to them? Was it all a wild goose chase and speculation? He would still suggest it to the lawyers and see what they thought. Perhaps the title was not as clear as they had thought and there was a battle of the estates. He was out of his depth.

The door slammed. Nicholas heard Nadia say, "Darling, are you there?"

"In the study, dear," he answered promptly.

"I see. There you are. Surely you cannot be working this time of the evening. Come out. I will tell you all about my evening."

"Sure. In a minute, dear. I am just about to draft an email."

"Can't it wait? There is so much to say about the class and my performance this evening."

"All right. I am coming, dear," he said obligingly.

Chapter 5

Blossoming Bouquets

In Surrey, Marguerite's garden was blooming. The aromas of the different spring flowers emanated from the garden, including the faint scent of the azaleas. It was still dewy as Marguerite took a morning stroll to examine the new growth. Lance had had a difficult evening. She prayed that his pain would subside over the next few weeks. The whole event had taken the joy out of the spring, and summer was fast approaching. Marguerite would use the memories of the past years to get her through this summer. There were so many, and the sacrifice of his recovery would be worth it. He was to be her priority, and now she felt alone. It was the news of the case again that had been haunting her. The Deneuve family had passed her mind some time ago, and the issue was now being revisited. With that came the memories of her father and, of course, Margaux. She wanted the issue over and buried.

Amelie examined the night jasmine by the French doors. Its aromas brought back idyllic memories. She knew that Lars was preoccupied and put it down to work. She wanted to do all that she could to help him alleviate that burden.

"Darling, I have news," he said as he approached her in the garden. She grew worried, thinking that it was something bad about her uncle.

"Is it serious? What is the matter?" she responded.

"I've heard from London. The men are out and have access to travel to the UK."

"Are you certain? How could this be?"

"We are not sure. They may no longer be a risk, and the crime did not happen at home apparently. So there is nothing to hold them back. That being said, we can still issue personal restraining orders, but it would be hard based on the grounds."

"But we will try, right?"

"Yes, we will. At least your family will. There is nothing to worry about. We can stay another week. There is no need to get back until the end of June, right?" he responded, comforting her.

"I suppose. However, I've missed so much already. This is really dampening my spirits and is not anything like how I thought my summer would pan out."

"Do not worry. We will sort it for you, Amy." The aroma of the jasmine grew dry as she walked, preoccupied, to the cottage. Lars walked beside her, not knowing what to do.

"How about a long tour of the island tomorrow? We can nip into town and do some shopping, have a bite to eat. What do you think?"

"Sounds perfect. But we must call London first. And I have to get some work done," she replied despondently.

"Sure, first thing in the morning," he promised.

It felt like the dawn to them as they had only been a few days out of the British summertime. She fell into a deep slumber for a bit and then, once she awoke, worked on her iPad. Mitch was planning a trip to South Africa and needed scheduling and consulting. Lars was just turning over and about to rise.

"Coffee, dear? I can make some."

"That would be lovely. I just want to finish this booking, and then we can call Nicholas."

"Sure, and then we probably need to call Roger, but we can hear what Nicholas has to say."

"Yes, perfect," she answered optimistically.

"Would you like some mangoes or tangerines?"

"Lovely, darling."

"Here we go then." He passed her the breakfast.

"Lovely, thank you."

They took a few sips. Then he picked up the phone and put it on speaker as he dialled.

Nicholas picked up. "Hello."

"Hello, Dad, how are you?"

"Fine, thank you, dear. How are you?"

"Great. Lars and I want to discuss what is happening."

"I see. How are your grandparents?"

"Lovely. Nan wants to see you soon, I think. She asked when you would be coming."

"I think later in the summer. Lars, how are you?"

"I am fine, thanks. We just want to get some more information. We think that we will stay a few more weeks here. It puts the rest of the summer in jeopardy as I have work to catch up on, but under the circumstances, I think that Amy deserves a bit of a break."

"I firmly agree. Now, Amelie, do not worry. We are working on it from here. Hank is talking to the solicitor, and we still plan to go ahead with the orders. However, they are searching for the ringleaders. I have no idea; it may be something from Grandpapa's days, so I am just going to get an investigator to look into it. I am sure the authorities are on it, but they may have overlooked the issue as it was so long ago."

"Well, Dad, what is it?"

"Well, there was meant to be a sale that fell through. Your grandfather decided to keep half the lot now worth forty-five million euros. At the time of his will, he left the whole bit to your aunt and mother in trust so that, if need be, it could be in a gallery. We need to figure out who is behind that and if there is any connection to the sale that went awry. In other words, someone else might be claiming their rights in having decided to steal the art."

"It all sounds so complicated. I am so lost about this."

"Sorry, dear. It is just that there is such a personal air to it all, and it implies someone with particular knowledge."

"I see. How horrid. I feel so much better," she said sarcastically.

"Now, now, dear, you just stay put and then come back when we have cracked this. It just needs a bit of investigating. The legal team are on it, dear. It is just that you are a beneficiary and could be in jeopardy. To avoid anything, just stay put or take another trip. These activities happen every year. You will only miss one or two. You will be back for Henley and the tennis," Nicholas consoled her.

"Yes, Amy. I could not agree more. It will be fine. I may need to get back to London for a few days and come back, or we can go to the South of France. It is where you feel safest."

"I will have to see. I would prefer to be with Nan. Aunt Marguerite is busy, so it will be lonely in France."

"OK. I am sure Mum would love having you. Try to be affable, dear."

"Of course I will. I love it here with them and Verena," she protested.

"I know, dear. I know. Now I must get moving on this. I will get back to you in a few days with the updates. I am not really a legatee in the matter, but Hank will be involved. It just crossed my mind all of a sudden," he explained.

"Thank you, Nick. Take care. We will hear from you soon. Bye," added Lars.

"Yes, Dad, bye—and speak to you soon."

"Bye-bye." Nicholas hung up.

Amelie stretched to reduce the stress.

"That is a perfect idea. Let's go for a jog on the beach," Lars suggested.

"All right then. I could use some exercise. I guess I'd better get back into my regime since I will be spending more time here."

"Yes, we'll take it all in stride, dear," he reassured her.

"You are always so understanding during these times, which are happening far more often, I must admit."

"Not to worry. Now shall we go on that invigorating jog on the beach?"

"Sure. That would really make me feel better."

Nicholas hung up, warier than ever. The more he spoke and thought about it, the more likely it all became. He had not suspected until it was said that there was someone else involved who might be more closely associated with the family than expected. Uncertain of what to do, he called Hank.

"Hello. I have just spoken to Amelie, and she is not that good, I suppose."

"I see. I suppose it is to be expected now that there is more investigating to do."

"Yes. Have you got Roger on it?"

"Certainly. How about your private eye?"

"He is making a journey to France as we speak. He will be heading down south to investigate the gallery and its owners. Who would have thought that they had their intentions on the whole lot all along?"

"I know. I thought that the deal was over and done with. Really, when Grandpapa changed his mind over the sale and withdrew, I thought that it was the final shot," added Hank.

"I guess that we were wrong. But to attempt something so unthinkable is beyond me."

"Absolutely preposterous the way that this is all panning out."

"Unthinkable to imagine. What your poor mother would have been going through had she lived to see this," observed Nicholas.

"What could they possibly want? Do you think that they will relent?" asked Hank.

"I think so. I am glad that we caught it in time. When Amelie went to clear out the deposit box, that caused an alarm."

"Yes. It certainly did. Otherwise, we would have never seen the paintings again," reasoned Hank.

"Surely. Never again," concluded Nicholas.

Meanwhile, Mr Hoover had travelled to the South of France to meet the head of the DeClementis family who owned the gallery. He was the partner of the late Guillaume Deneuve, who'd had the contract with Louis, Margaux's father.

"Good afternoon, Mr Hoover," he greeted. "What brings you to the Continent so abruptly?"

"I am afraid I am on business for a private client who has a lot at stake," responded Mr Hoover.

"In what way? This is a reputable establishment. We have been in operation for almost a century. My father and his partner first opened in the early part of the last century. What seems to be the problem?" he enquired.

"The problem is that a batch of paintings were almost taken from the estate of the late Margaux Mullbury. The culprits were found, but not the ringleader. It is now speculated that the ringleader could be someone they once knew. It is my job to find out who."

"Well, I understand your concern. Would this not be something for the authorities? And what would you want with me?" he contested.

"I do not think that it is you, but maybe you can help us assess who it is not. My client wants to rule out the possibility that it is something to do with this establishment and your late partner. Did he have any beneficiaries of his estate?"

"Well, his son, Jude, took over and has been living ... I am not sure. The last time we heard, he was in Lausanne. However, I am not sure. I do believe that he travels often. You can read that as you may."

"Thanks for that information. Did you have any further dealings with the Mullbury family before your partner died?"

"Not me personally. However, I am aware that Clyde did try to purchase the paintings again, but the contract no longer stood up in court, I believe. Now if that is all, I have a business to attend to."

"Thank you for speaking with me. I will not waste any more of your time. It has been a pleasure talking with you. I am sure that my client will be pleased."

"Perfect. Can I show you the way out?"

"Thank you. Have a nice day."

Mr Hoover was pleased with his progress. Although Mr DeClementis was brief and abrupt, he got the feeling that there was nothing to hide. His main focus was on the son, Jude, in Lausanne. It was what they had been suspecting all along. There was more to investigate. His next trip was to Switzerland.

Nicholas and Hank awaited the news and were upset to hear it. Now it was certain that Margaux's and Louis's past had come back to haunt them, and it would bring up more memories which had up to this point settled with time. They were unaware that there was more to the attempted heist as they waited for more information that could assist the authorities. There was a sense of unease but not necessarily anger. An acute form of deceit had been attempted, and they felt vulnerable. They decided not to tell Amelie until they knew more and were certain.

They made a call to Roger, who took news of the progress with alarm. There had been new players added to the case who were undetected from the beginning. It made him wonder if the culprits knew who had been backing them from the beginning. If not, then it was a much larger ring than expected, and there was too much uncertainty for anyone to feel safe. He knew for certain that Amelie could not be the culprit. Neither could anyone else in the family. He rushed through with the plans to ensure a rapid halt of any form of contact before Amelie and Lars travelled. It was a good guess that they would be trying to come back to finalise anything that might have been left incomplete.

For Nicholas, it became even more unbearable. He could imagine himself telling Margaux that everything was going to be fine. Memories began to swarm in his mind, youthful ones of her during the summers in a linen dress packing a picnic to take to the park, when her life was full and her father was still alive. He remembered her discussing the intended plan for the paintings and how her father had decided against it. He looked through the files to ensure that he had the proof. The main witnesses were gone, and evidence had declined. He also wanted to prevent anyone from concocting the evidence.

He heard the front door from his den.

"Darling, are you there?" asked Nadia.

"Yes, dear. I am down here," he answered.

"Lovely. I had a fabulous time at rehearsals, dear."

"Splendid. It has been a bit of an awkward day."

"Really? What is the matter?" she asked.

"Not much. Just some news about the case from Mr Hoover. No need to worry," he answered reassuringly.

"Oh. I see. Well, the play is in six weeks. I hope that it won't be too hectic for you to come to see."

"No, no. Not at all. It will be perfect, and I am looking forward to seeing it. You have been working so hard."

"I know. I am beat every evening. We have been rehearsing for weeks. But you will enjoy the final production. Just think, a year ago, I would not have thought that I would be back onstage."

"No, certainly not. Whatever makes you happy, dear. We cannot wait to see the production."

"Thanks. It means so much to me that you are so supportive. Now I am going to sort dinner for us."

"Sure, dear. I will be right up. I need a break from it all."

He was worried that he might be a key witness as there were so few people left who knew about the case. Marguerite was so busy; this would be the last thing she needed while Lance was convalescing. She was so preoccupied, and this news would only upset her.

Marguerite was resting in her lawn chair. It had been a full week of convalescence for Lance. Her whole order of life had turned, and she found herself again appreciating the most basic things. It was a fresh late spring day with the flowers blooming even more. Lance was indoors so as not to catch the evening draught. These were quiet moments that she spent alone to keep sane. His chemo was almost finished with only a few more weeks to go. He was often very sick. She had a hired nurse, Bridget, who looked after him. By this time, Marguerite would have been at the summer galas. Now it did not faze her that she would not be attending. All the invitations had fallen by the wayside.

Her phone rang. It was Hank.

"Hello, dear. How are you?"

"Rather well, considering. How are you both doing?"

"I am well. Your uncle is taking longer than expected to get used to the chemo."

"I am sorry to hear about him. Do please send him our love."

"Of course. Every day he knows. He cannot wait to get back to his normal self."

"Fantastic. I do not mean to be a bit of a bother; Amelie has decided to stay at Nan's, and we think it best."

"Definitely. It is the safest choice until we get over this news. It is horrid. To think that it could be connected to that situation years ago. Daddy never went through with it. I do not know what they may have to do to prove that he did. Regardless, they should not have gone through such channels. Who do you think is ultimately involved?"

"I do not know. Dad is looking at old documents, and there is a private investigator on it who is travelling to Switzerland."

"I see," she responded despondently. "With all that I have to worry about, this is so disconcerting."

"I know. It really is not the right time. And Amelie is now stuck on the island for the season. Hopefully she will be back by July for the tennis. We have been popping in to look at their place, and Mildred and Marietta are checking on the flat in London. It has been a disaster. And then the legal predicaments of getting those people far away from us! We had hoped that they would stay far away, and then they got out early and won't talk."

"I know. Maybe they are not safe either. It is all sounding like a big conspiracy. I hope that it all gets resolved before something else happens," she reasoned.

"Well, that is precisely why I have called. It is a warning to be cautious. I know that you are busy with Uncle, but we have to be wary. I can check on the paintings for you in France and warn the guardians that there may be trouble and to be especially cautious," answered Hank.

"Fabulous. Please do take care of it. We won't get back until the end of the summer. I would hate for something else to happen."

"Lovely. Have a wonderful evening. Jenny and the children are waiting for me to have dinner. Bye."

"Bye, my dear. And I will give Lance your love." She hung up. She felt more secure that he had called. He was such a dear nephew who always had a kind heart and looked after her. He was her hope if something were to happen to Lance. She preferred not to think about it, however. She could smell the night jasmine, and it reminded her of when they used to get ready to have dinner. Bridget appeared to inform her that the meal was ready.

They were cautious of what they ate, especially now, and the summer produce was ideal. Marguerite ensured that her husband had lots of greens and fresh dairy with omega-3 fish and fresh berries. There was always fish for dinner, followed by probiotics and tea. She used any remedy that she could to get him better. The medicine had him nauseous, and she hoped that he could retain some nutrients. She was exhausted and hoped for the best.

Chapter 6

Sunny Landscapes

It was still just past lunchtime for Amelie, who used the day to catch up on work. She had been on the phone and on her computer for most of the morning. She and Lars had a light lunch with Winnie and Lionel, and Lars decided to have a swim to burn some calories. Amelie completed the arrangements with Mr Mitchvale and had been on the phone to her assistant in London. She was still downcast about the news from London.

"I have never heard of those people whom Dad referred to earlier," she said, perplexed, to Lars.

"It is as if there has been such an unknown for most of my life. To think that someone targeted me. It is so unthinkable. I am thankful to be here until they get this all sorted. The only thing is that I am missing all the events this summer."

"Not all. Just some until we get the injunctions together. I am very sorry that it has not panned out the way that you want it to. Everyone in London, from your family to Lydia and Lorraine, think that this is best until we know more. Mr Hoover is in Switzerland and is checking on the Deneuve chap. It should all be revealed. I miss London too as it has been just over two weeks that we have been here."

"It is not good for my business. I am not even there."

"I know. We should give it another week or two, and then it should be safer. Why don't we go to the resort for dinner and dancing on Saturday night? It will be fabulous," he suggested.

"Certainly. It would be divine. Something else to look forward to while I wait," she complied.

"Sure, and there should be more of the locals on Saturday to hang out with again. It will be as if we are young again."

"Certainly." She grew optimistic. She had fond memories of being a young woman on the island and part of the social scene. She used to celebrate with the locals and had become close to those families in the vicinity. Sadly, so many had moved off and had families of their own. She was a bit of a late bloomer, but now she had Lars to escort her everywhere. She grew excited at the thought of going to the old haunts. It started with pizza parlours with groups of friends and then perusing the casinos with the same friends as a young woman. Then she'd attended the clubs as a university graduate. And recently there was the New Year's Eve celebration with her family. That memory was not so memorable, though. It was the evening of the attempted heist, and they had returned after a wonderful evening only to find out that there had been a crime committed back home and in France. Her life had changed. This was the most that she had grown since then. Now it all felt like déjà vu.

"Yes. Like the old days."

"Lars, I feel as though something is about to happen again," she admitted.

"Don't be silly. We will have a lovely time. Nothing will happen. You will see."

"Let's hope that you are right. I think that it will be lovely to go to the resort like in the old days."

"Why don't we take a long stroll on the beach? Just us? Come on. Shall we?" He stood and offered his arm. She complied.

"Sure. Just let me find my trainers, and we'll be off to the beach." She giggled, trying to keep her spirits high.

They started a long walk as the sun dipped to the afternoon position. The shoreline had receded to low tide. They walked out to the centre of the bay. They waded their feet in the water until they were knee high.

"It is amazing that we can do this and go so far out."

"Yes. Any boat would scrape the bottom without proper navigation," observed Lars.

"That's right. When we were younger there were smaller boats in the area—only fishing boats. Mum and I would walk the shoreline and collect seashells."

"Right. Shall we then? Collect seashells?"

She was pleased and laughed. "Of course."

They wandered along the shore, trying to collect whatever they could. Amelie was miles away from her disaster at home. It felt as though they were in another world and the past was now a dream. She was again in her safe place and optimistic.

"It is almost time for dinner," she commented.

"Right. Let's head back." They turned and navigated towards the house. They had been walking for almost an hour.

Mr Hoover's country train stopped in the small town. He took a taxi to an art gallery in the centre of town. He was looking for a Mr Jude Deneuve, the grandson of Guillaume and heir to his estate.

The chateau was enchanting in the centre of town. He inspected the work that was hung in the gallery and came across some medieval artwork from about the same period as the family collection. *How coincidental,* he thought.

"May I help you?" a voice asked conspicuously.

"I am actually looking for Mr Deneuve. Can you tell me where to find him?"

"Who might I say is asking?" He looked suspiciously.

"It is Mr Hoover. I am a private investigator from London. I am calling about the Mullbury family and some art."

"Just a moment. I will see if he is available."

Mr Hoover waited in the foyer and soon was led to the office of Jude.

"My, you have gone down memory lane. Now, Mr Hoover, how can I help you?" he asked.

"I am pleased to make your acquaintance. Thank you for seeing me."

"Well, the name rings a bell. They are old friends of the family. Louis and Guillaume were business associates, some might say rivals, but I have a different perspective as memories mellow with time."

"Well, there was an attempted heist of the Mullbury collection, and now I know that there is a ringleader. I don't suppose that you could tell me a bit about the sentiment over the family collection."

"Well, I do not know much, and of course it was a long time ago. The paintings were meant to be sold for the gallery. My grandfather specialised in that type of art, and there was a contract which was not followed through fully. I do not know what happened after that."

"Can you tell me more, like the amount?"

"I do believe at the time it was today's value of fifteen million euros. I am sure the paintings are worth more, but I do not know," he answered vaguely.

"I see. Yes, they are now worth about forty-five million euros—approximately thirty million to forty million at the time of the heist."

"I see. I would not know the figures. You are telling me this now," he admitted.

"How did your grandfather feel about the broken contract?"

"I am not too sure. There may have been legal proceedings. I am sure they negotiated a sum in the end as people do when there are broken promises."

"I see. Do you think that it would have been sufficient?"

"I cannot say. It was some time ago. The money was in francs and would have a different value today. Whether he was happy? I would say not. He had banked on the sale and made other dealings in reliance, which fell through."

"When you say other dealings, do you have any idea with whom?"

"I have no idea. It would be in his documents, which are securely tucked away now. There was interest, and he had another sale relying on the paintings. However, it never came to pass. I do believe that they are still with the family?"

"Yes, you are right. The Mullburys are concerned because there is someone else out there, and they do not want it to happen again. Did your father try to purchase the paintings again?"

"I cannot remember. Again, it was some time ago. He may have approached them. ... Well, anything more and you will have to contact me through my lawyers. Here is the card where they are available. I am sorry that I cannot be of any more help. Do have a nice day, Mr Hoover."

"I thank you for your time. It has helped immensely."

"Whatever I can do. Now I have other appointments."

"Have a nice day." Mr Hoover left and felt as though he had made some progress. It was not a wasted journey, and he gotten a sense that there was a third party, namely the other people who were relying on the sale. Going though attorneys would be hostile, and he wanted to rule out Deneuve. Could he? Were those people pressuring him to come up with the goods? Was he involved? It was getting deeper. Hoover had found his point of call. But were they all involved? He phoned Hank with the updates.

"Yes, hello. I have just finished the meeting here in Lausanne, and I have news. I did speak to Jude Deneuve, and I think that he knows a bit more about his father's dealings. He has given me his lawyer's card if we need anything more. He did say that there were third parties involved relying on the sale. We now need to find out what happened to them."

"Thank you. That is good news. Great job. I think that we can go to Roger with this. Once we find the third party, we can go to the authorities with it. It is all seeming a bit suspicious now."

"That is right. I get the feeling that we are on the right track."

Meanwhile, Jude decided to make a call. "I got a visitor from the Mullbury family. He was asking about the sale. I do not think that he knows anything. I assessed him, and he was fishing for information. I will get back to you if there is anything else."

"I see. It is strange that they would enquire now. It has been years. Just keep me posted," added Mr Gouter.

"OK. Do you think that she will remember you?"

"I do not know. It was long ago, and we never met."

"All right. Perfect."

"I suppose that it is because Shadrock and Mesnel are out. We can't get a hold of them either."

"Will they talk?"

"I don't think so. They do not want to go back to where they came from, do they?"

"Bye."

He hung up.

Amelie felt as though the week had been productive even though she was on the outskirts of her regular routine. There was something alluring about having a portable office on an island during her vacation. Her life was centred in Knightsbridge, and it was a refreshing change. She suddenly missed the sounds of the rattling engines of the taxis passing and the aroma of food from the trendy cafes. It was her part of town as it had been for years. She looked across to the patio's courtyard and tried to glance in through the French doors to the sitting room. She could see her grandmother's figure sitting and reading the magazines and papers. This also was a normal sight for Amelie when on vacation. It was such an idyllic vacation environment.

However, when Amelie was growing up, Winifred's lifestyle had been very different. Amelie had distant and protracted memories of her grandmother as a business woman in her boutique. She and Margaux would walk down to a bazaar filled with stores in the centre of town where the store was located. She anticipated seeing her figure dressed to the nines and seated in an elaborate chair behind a delicately carved white desk which held a cash register and ledgers. Her excitement grew not only to see her Nan, but also to wander through the store, which appeared massive and was filled with colourful, glistening merchandise and racks of clothing within which she could get lost. She was still small enough that she could get lost behind the clothes on the racks. She remembered the aroma of fresh fabric and carpeting. Items were shipped in from all over the world, including France, New York, and London.

It was a cutting-edge boutique which dressed the most affluent in island society. Amelie would always want to stay and play with Winifred, who was very busy at work. Often customers would come in, and Winifred's carefully trained assistants would assist them. She was a very crafty saleswoman, and her staff were just as astute. They would often work overtime, unpacking boxes of inventory for the shelves each season. As the business expanded, so did the amount of inventory that had to be calculated. Sometimes Amelie did not have to wait to travel to see her grandmother because the latter would often come to London to buy merchandise from popular fashion houses. Winifred was well versed with the trade and with the exhausting practice of shipping. However, it was worth the joy that she saw on her customers' faces when she would remove designer gowns from their coverings and show them to clients. Winifred was always sophistically dressed and would often save items for Amelie when she came to town to wear to the galas at the resort and to church.

Margaux would let Winifred take over the dressing, and Amelie would wear designer frocks, matching accessories and stockings, and delicate coloured jewellery from the boutique. She bestowed a sense of style that could only be seen on the Continent or Fifth Avenue. Times had changed since then, and they were all more relaxed amid the changing practices and evolution of style. Winifred was more mellow and not as cutting edge; however, still reminisced on those days and still assessed everything that her granddaughter wore. She often wished that she'd had a daughter of her own so that the boutique would have remained in the family. However, a successful sale of the chain made her comfortable for her winter years. Her style went with Amelie, who lived in a very fashionable part of London, with Margaux being popular in Knightsbridge. She'd been raised among a sophisticated sort of precision in the fashion world. Now she made her style very tailored yet comfortable with a slight flair. It did not mean that she did not appreciate the type of extravagance such as in the boutique, just that it was always around her. She went to the closet to pick out an outfit to wear to the resort casino that evening. Her choices were limited as she was running out of clothes.

Lars would soon be back from a few errands in town, and they were to head straight to the restaurant and then enjoy a night on the town. She wanted to be ready when he arrived.

"I am back. It is very warm out. My, you look lovely. I like that on you," he commented as he greeted her with a kiss.

"Thank you. I was running out of things to wear. How was your outing?"

"Fantastic. I wanted to get back in time. Let me dash to the loo and freshen up before we head out. We should make it there before happy hour ends."

"Sure. I will be here." She turned on the cable TV and flicked through the channels, which were all US channels. She found a few reruns and turned to the news.

Within moments, Lars stepped out wearing a clean polo shirt and khakis. "Is this fine?" he asked.

"Great for a Friday night out. What about that cologne I bought?"

"Thanks. I'll just put some on." Her having been brought up by a French mother and amid Winfred's traditions made her emphasise cologne. *Less is more*, she could remember Margaux saying.

"Not too much, dear," she advised.

"OK, are we ready? How do I smell?" he asked as he leaned over.

"Perfect. Let's go and say bye to Nan like we are going on a proper date," she suggested.

"Sure. Like the early years."

"Gosh, I remember when I would invite you down and you and my brother would share the cottage. Those were the days of sneaking about. Let's now go and create more memories."

Lars escorted her to the French doors, which opened onto the different world of her grandparents and all their memories. He was just relieved that she was not thinking about the case, because the news from London was not good. It was all looking like a set-up, and there were more people involved—people who had targeted her.

They hopped in the convertible and drove to the resort with the wind blowing through her bobbed blonde hair that had been lightened by the sun. The resort was appealing as they drove nearer. She savoured the nightlife that awaited them.

"I cannot believe that we are finally having a date night at our old haunt. How long has it been?" she observed.

"I think since we got married. Or just before," he responded.

"I think you are right. It has been a long time. Well, let us see what the others are saying. I have not seen anyone in so long."

The valet took the car after they disembarked. Then they walked through the casino to the restaurants overlooking the water.

"Superb. Splendid view," he remarked.

"Lovely. So romantic," she responded as she took the menu. "It is not too late," she said, surveying the place as people were still crowding around the bar areas and enjoying the afternoon before the weekend.

"Do you recognise anyone?"

"Not really," she responded. "I suppose that they will come in sooner or be at the Promenade later, the newest nightlife venue."

"Yes. Probably later."

"I cannot believe that we are still here. We have just left everything and come here," she stated.

"Don't worry. We will soon be back. Now, let's think about to-night. What are you having?"

"I have not had the fritters in a while. Shall we order a plate?"

"Go for it. Also, some daiquiris? They are so tropical here."

"Great suggestion," she replied.

The evening lingered as they sipped their drinks and savoured the fritters.

"Anything else?"

"Yes. Let's get some of the coconut cream pie. Remember that?" she responded.

"How can I forget?"

"Or would you prefer the key lime pie?"

"One slice of each. I will help you, promise."

"Thanks. I have never been able to choose between the two when I am here."

"No. I suppose not," he joked.

"Ha ha, very funny." She grew bemused.

"Is that Kerry? That looks like Kerry and Dave," he observed.

"Where?"

"Over there." He motioned.

"I see. Yes. That is them. Shall we go over to say hello?"

"Sure. I am sure that they will be at the Promenade later."

"Yes. I am sure." They gazed at the ocean as the lights brightened and the sun dipped below the horizon. The lights from the building now glistened on the water, which had grown deeper.

Lars did not want to detract from this moment. Things were about to take a turn, and Amelie would soon be forced to go down memory lane and revisit what happened a few years ago. He did not want to distract her from this perfect evening.

In Bedfordshire, Hank tossed and turned as he thought about the developments and solutions. He was a man who fixed things and took control. He wanted to take control of the situation. First, they needed to requisition Jude and DeClementis and then find out who they knew. The evidence was mounting as Mr Hoover was working very hard. He felt as though Shadrock and Mesnel would no longer be a problem. Once they found out that something else had been discovered, they would not want to return to the UK. He would ask Roger to get the lawyers in Switzerland to work on the matter.

"What's the matter, dear?" asked Jenny.

"Just thinking about that issue," Hank confided.

"I see. Do not worry. It will work itself out," she reassured him.

"I do not know why this is still going on."

"It will soon be over, you will see. The lawyers are working on it. Now get some rest."

"They are. Thanks, dear." He succumbed to her suggestion, still unsure.

"You can deal with it on Monday. Right now, just try to relax," she coaxed him.

"Thanks." He pretended as if he adhered to her advice, but it was no use. With every minute, there was a chance that something would happen—even more now since they knew that someone was onto the culprits.

Amelie and Lars watched the sunset while they sipped a rich authentic aged Malbec. The Promenade Club had proven quite adventurous. They still were amazed by how much the social scene had progressed since they began dancing. It was late, almost 11 p.m.

"Have you ever stayed here?"

"No. Must be fabulous upstairs," Amelie responded.

"We have a suite ready. I booked it last week."

"What? That is so thoughtful. I can't believe that you did that."

"I know. It is a surprise."

"Well, I am surprised. Let me text Nan to tell her that we are staying out."

"Sure. If you'd like. I did warn them just in case."

"Fabulous. I will just remind her. You know how much she worries."

He breathed in and smiled to himself. *Some things will never change,* he thought. It took him back to their early days when they were out and Winifred would command such control. He just let Amelie do it.

"Would you like another drink?"

"I am curious to see what the rooms are like. Shall we wander up?"

"All right. I'll just get the check, and we will be on our way."

He signed the bill, and they ventured up to the suite that had an aquatic theme.

"It is beautiful. I have never been in this one. I know we booked a few for the guests for our wedding. This is superb," Amelie commented as she inspected the rooms. Then she went to the balcony. "Splendid view, isn't it?"

"Lovely," he said as he slipped his arm around her waist. They watched the boat lights travelling up the harbour.

"Thank you. This is so thoughtful. A lovely break within a break."

"You're more than welcome, dear. Anything for you. Shall we order some Moët?"

"Wonderful idea. I am a bit peckish. Perhaps some cheese? All of that dancing—I must have burned a few calories."

"Sure thing. Coming right up," he joked.

"I feel so safe and away from it all. I had completely forgotten about all that mess with the case tonight. This was the perfect idea."

"I know. That is what I intended. And you got to see a few familiar faces."

"That is right. We should try to meet up with Kerry and Dave again before we leave. We should invite them out on the boat. It was delightful catching up with everyone."

"I know. Let's invite them out. Remember, we are flying out soon—next weekend. It will have to be soon."

"Yes. With a little bit of luck we shall be back for the Ascot and tennis."

"That is right, dear. That is right."

They sat engaged by their surroundings, sipping the champagne and eating hors d'oeuvres.

"This is beautiful," she said, pleased that he'd been so precise in his planning.

"It is, dear. It is."

Nadia toned her voice for her rehearsal. Warming up was the starting point, and then came voice and breathing. Her diaphragm was being overworked again, and precision was key. She stretched and then went over her lines in a quiet place before the rehearsals. It was a musical about a group of factory workers in a plant in the Midlands before the demise of the industry. They were in their heyday with a 1930s motif and spinning bright fabrics to make suits and gowns. The finale was the glamorous gala at the ballroom in the town centre, which happened each year. Nadia wore a factory uniform and had a supporting role of a worker whose husband was migrating to New York for work after the plant closed.

She identified with the conflict in her character after her choice to restart work at the theatre after such a long hiatus and her own personal conflict. The musical was set to run this fall. She had anticipated that the case would all be over by then as Nicholas had been so preoccupied. She had not seen him so worried in years.

"Everyone, get prepared and step onto the stage," ordered the director. "We will start with Act II at the factory. Bea, you start with your line 'What do they think that we will all do after the plant closes?' Then we will sing, 'Wish It Was Yesterday'. Am I clear?"

The company nodded and got to their positions.

BEA What do they think that all these people will do after they close now?

NADIA I haven't a clue. I have a young baby and my mister is looking to move to New York.

BEA What? New York? What are you going to do without him?

NADIA I have no idea. He says that I should go with him.

BEA With him? And take the baby there too?

NADIA That's right? Now you see what a position I am in, now that my life has changed. If only it could be yesterday," she responded.

"Perfect, everyone. You have done a good job," said the director. "So now we are going to take it from Act III. Do tell me that you all know the lines and then the finale."

They all scrambled to their places for the next scene as the rehearsal went on. Nadia felt invigorated by the role and was caught up in the moment as she said her lines and sprang into dance and song. She hoped that her family could come and watch as soon as the issue was over.

Hank called Nicholas, who had been rummaging through old documents.

"Hello, Dad. How are you?"

"Fine. I am just looking to see if your mother had anything to help with the case. There must be something regarding the reneged sale. You see, if they are working on the premise that there could be a sale still in place and that they are entitled to the paintings, then it is a new point. This could throw the whole thing out of sorts and put the ownership in question. What horrid people we are dealing with."

"I know. It is all so sinister and calculated. It is as if they had this planned all along. Whoever they are."

"That is right, whoever they are. From Mr Hoover I gather that it could be a few of them working together and that their eyes were on the paintings."

"What they could not get legally, they decided to steal. I will not have the family assets destroyed in this way. There must be a solution, and whoever is responsible needs to be brought to justice. I propose that the Swiss lawyers serve them with documents to get them to acknowledge that there is no ownership and that the deal was buried years ago. Once they admit to it, we should not have anything to worry about. If they refuse, then it is up to the authorities, as it may have been all along."

"That is a good idea. I will see if there is any more from Hoover. I think that he was going to dig a bit deeper before returning. He suspects that they are hiding something."

"Right then. We will see what he has to say."

"Fabulous. Talk to you soon. And try not to worry about it all. It is under control."

"Righty-ho, Dad."

Amelie and Lars awoke to the sounds of the waves and the sight of the boats on the harbour. They sat on the balcony and watched the sunrise. They had a sensible night and were not too exhausted from the drinks and dancing.

"Croissants, dear, and some coffee?"

"Splendid, a lovely breakfast on the balcony. You have truly thought about everything. Do we get a late checkout?"

"Sure. At least 1 p.m., I think."

"Good. I am not in a rush to get back to the cottage. We should have an afternoon wander on the promenade. We never know who we might bump into."

"That is a good idea. I just feel like a smoothie and banana this morning. We had so much yesterday."

"I know." She grinned.

They ordered and peacefully sipped and savoured the breakfast over the ocean's view. It was going to be sweltering. Her mind slipped back to a cool summer breeze and the deep, damp earth of the countryside. She yearned for her cottage in the countryside and the bustle of Knightsbridge, but she would not dare let Lars know. They lounged around and walked the beach before packing their things in the convertible and heading back to the house.

"Lovely break, wasn't it?" he asked as he drove around the bend back to the house.

"Fabulous. I think that we should stay again if it will not insult Nan."

"Great idea. Next time we shall spend a weekend and then spend time with her."

"Perfect." They were meant to return with more family at the end of the summer. "I hope that the case will be over by then."

"Certainly ..." he reassured her.

When they arrived, Winnie and Lionel were having lunch in the wicker sitting room.

"Well, did you have a nice break?" Winifred asked as they walked in the door.

"We sure did. It was wonderful. They have really upgraded that hotel," Amelie replied.

"Great news. Are you hungry? Verena has made some fish salad and banana bread," she offered.

"Thanks. I could have something," negotiated Lars.

"Perfect. We shall come right out after we have dropped these things in the back," resolved Amelie.

They headed to the cottage, where they dumped their bags and freshened up before heading back out again. They joined the luncheon and tucked into their meal.

Chapter 7

Continental Days

Mr Hoover decided to stay a few extra days in Zurich. He still had a piece of the puzzle that needed to be figured out. DeClementis had worked with Deneuve in the 1970s and was meant to purchase the paintings from Grandfather Louis, who withdrew the offer and the contract. They assumed that Louis was in breach of contract and wanted compensation. Whatever they received was not enough to get them out of the bind that they were already in with a third seller. The third party could have paid money, which he felt gave him a right to the paintings or a portion of the proceeds. Who was the seller, and who was the buyer? Hoover went back to the original theft. Whom was the gang working for, and to whom were they selling? It was becoming a maze. The answer relied on who was Deneuve selling to in breach of the contract. Why did they still want the paintings?

Jude sat in his office and went over the documents of the initial sale. It was clearly for the named Renaissance paintings and between Louis and his grandfather Guillaume. Later there was a breach of contract and then another contract signed by Mr Linx and his father, Clyde. There was also correspondence between Margaux and

Clyde where she renounced the sale after the paintings were assigned to Louis's estate. Clyde never thought that she had the right as she was not the original beneficiary of the sale but was a new owner acting on behalf of the estate. He knew deep down what Clyde would have done, and it was not legitimate. Now he was left to sort this, and he had only the word of Mr Gouter. All the others were deceased. Jude assumed that it was Mr Linx or his estate with an interest in the paintings.

"What can you tell me about Linx?" he asked Gouter.

"He was a partner in a merchant bank and wanted the paintings to diversify the portfolio of a client. DeSabulus and Co. was the name of the bank, and it operated abroad. His partner is also deceased, and his son Knot inherited the bank back in 1985."

"Do you think that he is behind this corporate veil?"

"Perhaps. Or the client. It is difficult to say. No one will talk. And now if we do not find out, everyone will think that we had something to do with it. I knew that this would happen. I wanted to warn Mullbury, but it was too late. I could not risk that appointment to tell her."

"It will look as if you are left with the bag unless we reveal Linx. How much did he stand to lose from the sale?"

"I am not sure. Perhaps fifteen million euros. He must have placed it in the portfolio. And the client needed to the appreciation of the assets, but there were none to be found."

"Perhaps. It is all water under the bridge, but it gives motive. I do not think that the gang even knew who they were working for."

"I do not think that they could trace it that far."

"I think that I can have my lawyer contact Hoover. I think that it would take the heat off me if we reveal this information."

"Whatever. Just be careful. If they have done it once, they can do it again. They can even put the blame on you."

"Right you are. They can blame anyone, and we do not know if they are to blame. But they are closer than we are to the sale. I do not wish to be embroiled in any lawsuit, yet they still do. This is an old case. I think that they are to blame for this mess. The sooner that we reveal, them the better."

"Yes. From my experience working with your father at the firm, things do not end well when this is involved and there is so much money at stake. Mullbury will come looking. He has already hired that private investigator. We had better have something for him."

"You are right. You need to get the emphasis off us and onto them. They can handle the heat."

"I bet they can."

Jude hung up, ready to offer an olive branch. It was the right thing to do as the case had been over for years. Whatever the dealings, he wanted no part of it. He had worked too hard to make it, and nothing was going to sacrifice his hard work and the new direction he'd taken with the company. The main players were gone, so it would be difficult to get evidence. He did not want any part of it.

He picked up the phone to call his lawyer to get into contact with Hoover.

"I think that it is a good idea. It appears that the case has been going on for decades, and it must end. I wish that I had known sooner. We could have sorted this. I want to make sure that you do not appear as an accomplice or concealer, so we will have to have something signed to relieve you of liability—or else there will be a price to pay. We are uncertain if the merchant bank is claiming the assets. It could have done so for decades, making ownership difficult to ascertain as the main players are now gone. That would make you a defendant for them if they want to take action. It seems as though you are close to being revealed through Hoover anyway. I would not advise to just do nothing. They will get there and find the answers. I will contact Mr Hoover or his client Nicholas first thing in the morning. Whatever they choose to do is on them. I just want you to know the consequences. I am sure that they want to see the end of this as soon as you do. It will be fine. I am working on it."

"Thank you. I want out of this. I cannot take the chance, as I do not know what is at stake or what the bank could claim from the breach at this point. The paintings have appreciated in value based on phantom ownership."

"Yes. I think that there is no question that they still own the paintings. It is sad that the merchant bank would have considered them to be their assets. We need to get to the bottom of it."

"Thank you. I will wait to hear back from you tomorrow after you have spoken to Hoover."

"Sure. Talk to you then."

Jude felt slightly relieved. He could not believe that something so unresolved had been left for him to deal with. He could not stop the last attempt, but surely he could help with the next, anticipated issue.

Nicholas awaited more news from Mr Hoover. He was still in Switzerland.

"Right. Now we have more information from Jude. I hear that he is cooperating as there was a third-party buyer who might be of interest—Apparently the DeSabulus bank owners, a Knot Linx?"

"I have not heard of him or the bank. I will l have to refresh my memory by looking over some documents."

"I see. Well, apparently the sale was for about fifteen million euros, and they had some clients depending on it."

"Thanks. That is good news. I am sure that Hank will be happy to hear it. I wish that I knew who they were. Now I have a call from Hank. I will speak to you later."

He disconnected and answered his son's call.

"Hello, Dad. I have just heard that Jude's lawyers are going to negotiate with ours in Zurich. They say that he has information on a merchant bank and would like to absolve himself of any liability."

"I see. Why now, and why so late?"

"They did not say. I presume it was after his conversation with Hoover. All I know is that it is good news. Then Amy can finally come home. She seems truly bored and would like to get back to her business. Our lives will be back to normal, and then we can just sort out whom to restrain from us and clear the title of our estate. It has been a complete nightmare, all this uncertainty."

"I know. The sooner the better. I would think that you would want to accommodate Jude and get him on your side. Now I am sure that Amy would love to hear the news. So I will check in on them later at Mum's. We can think of our travel later as she has been wondering when that will be after all this. Also, she can make it back in time for Wimbledon and the regatta. Cheerio."

"Cheerio," he replied.

The tiers of the investigation had deepened as Nicholas knew that they would. In this scenario, there were certainly always more players than initially assumed. It was not expected of the locale as this type of set-up was of a bygone era. How had it gone unnoticed for so long? Surely Margaux knew nothing about it—or did she? He would never know as she took it to her grave, and he could not bother her younger sister because she had so much to worry about. This all put him in a reflective mood on things unfinished and unaccounted for. It was now all as abrupt to him as the day he'd lost her. He shifted his mind to something more productive, like making plans at the club with Orry. It had been awhile. Perhaps Orry had heard of this mysterious bank.

Lydia was bemused that her friend had not returned to enjoy the summer with her. She thought to call and was aware that it was now later in the afternoon for Amelie.

"Hello. I am so glad that I have caught you. It appears it has been ages. How long are you down there?"

"Hi. Wonderful to hear from you. We were just finishing up a meal. Lars and I had a lovely weekend at the resort. I have been missing home and should be back soon."

"I see. How reassuring, because I thought that I lost you this summer. It is so boring here without you. And all of the parties are now in full swing."

"I know. It is such a bore that I must wait until that awful case is over. I think that there is more headway now. I could have been targeted. It is not safe for me to return until they have cracked it."

"Poor dear. I thought that they would have cracked it two years ago when it all happened. To think that it is just happening now."

"I know. All because Dad hired a private investigator. I so hope that this is the end of it and I can get back to life as normal. I really need to be with my aunt and, of course, my business. I am having to do things from here. Can't wait to see everyone. It must all be in full swing."

"Well, yes," she answered a bit apologetically.

"Are you sure?"

"Well, not really. There are still the races, the regatta, and tennis. Of course, the polo matches and everything are still abuzz in Knightsbridge for the summer as usual. You will see as it will not be long before you return."

"Right. I thought so. I might want to remain a bit low-key in the country and then go to France for a bit later in the summer, until this whole thing blows over and I can get those people away from me. Just think that I might have been contacted when we were at Clarence's place. Something is a bit eerie about the whole thing. It was so long ago that I cannot remember much."

"Not to worry. You have Lars, and you do not have to worry about it now. You have overcome so much. It will not affect you any more once this is over. Try to stay positive. Anyway, I almost miss your nan's cooking. It is a bit too late for us to come down."

"Yes. I think so. We will soon be back, hopefully by the end of next week. And I will be ready to get back on the scene. Mitchvale is heading to New York and Japan, and I am sorting that out for him. Also, my summer travellers have arrived, and they will be needing assistance at flats and outings, so I am missing so much. Luckily my assistant is doing a fantastic job. I don't suppose they know that I have left yet."

"Perfect. See you soon. We shall pop in once you are settled to have a coffee or something. You will see that this will soon be over."

"Thanks for your call. Chat soon." She felt more reassured.

"Yes. Chat soon, and take care." The two had been friends since public school, where Lydia had arrived at twelve years of age for boarding school. The two were more like family. Lydia was a very loyal friend. They had vacationed together since they were children with the Mullburys acting as the host family. It was unbearable for Lydia to see them going through such an ordeal. She wanted them out of their misery. Lydia had been the maid of honour when Amelie was married, and she'd helped Amelie through the first ordeal. She would be just as loyal now.

"That was Lydia. She wants us to get back now so that we can socialise this summer. She is right: I need to get back to work. I never thought that I would be bored."

"Not to worry. It will be all right. I have just received an email from Hank, and he says that they have cracked the case and one of the culprits will be negotiating. I think that we will be back in our little nest soon and going about our normal lives. I miss the gym, and I need to get to the office," Lars replied.

"I know, dear. I know," she answered compassionately.

The week on the island flew by. Amelie felt reticent about leaving her family, but she had so much to do back in London. She knew that she would see them again soon, as usual. The island was a special place she called home and was filled with wonderful memories of family and friends and of her wedding.

By Friday, the case had come along smoothly. Nicholas had thought that the last thing that he would have was another case to crack, but he was fully involved in protecting his family. It was what he had done all his life, and he would continue doing it whenever necessary. He went through his old documents and would be meeting Orry to get some more details on the old days. Time had flown, and memories had mellowed with the passing of time. He could feel the nostalgia of being in Mayfair and at one of Louis's diplomatic parties, where Margaux and Marguerite were dressed in the latest Marisa Martin or Mary Farrin designs of summer—the old days as he called them. He rummaged through the documents and found a letter to Clyde Deneuve denouncing the sale of the items. It was written by Margaux and offered the full and final settlement to withdraw from the contract.

"Hello, Hank. I've found the letter that we could put forward as evidence that there has not been any sale."

"That is good news. If you could, scan that over please. I got news from Roger from the lawyers in Switzerland, and the Deneuve lawyers have a waiver form to sign. I think that it would be in our best interests to concentrate on the culprits. I think they want to avoid liability."

"It might be a good idea to get more cooperation. Are they now concentrating on the Linx bank?" asked Nicholas.

"Yes. I think so. We should have this tied up by the time Amelie gets back, I think."

"Fabulous. You are all free of complications again. I hope that nothing else arises," confided Nicholas.

"Let's hope not," replied Hank.

"Great. Speak to you soon. I will have lunch with Orry, who might be able to refresh my memory some more."

"Right then. Have a nice lunch."

Nicholas left for a Friday afternoon lunch with Orry at the club. They had been friends since college and had worked as business associates a few times. Orry seemed to have a better recollection of the word on the street since he had been based in London for the entire time.

"Right then, old chap, what are you having?" Nicholas asked as they were seated.

Nicholas had cut down on his liquid lunches. However, since it was a Friday and it had been some time since they'd met, he decided to celebrate.

"Vodka Martini for me, thanks."

"Brandy for me," Orry told the waiter.

"So how are you all doing? Nadia? Amelie? Hank?"

"Great. Nadia is in a performance later this summer, and Amelie is flying in from Mum's tomorrow. Hank and I have been discussing the DeSabulus Bank. Do you remember it? I think that the Linx family might run it still?"

"Let me see. I am not sure that it rings a bell." Orry tried to jog his memory and thought back. "Why do you ask?"

"I am afraid it is a horrid mess over Margaux's family paintings. Apparently they were meant to be sold with Lou pulling out and then some other people still trying to claim them. I am sure there is a statute of limitations; however, it was some time ago that this bank had purported some ownership."

"Yes, it does sound like a horrid mess. Is this something to do with the case last year? I mean, are the two connected?"

"I think so. We were told that the people caught were working for someone else and there was a ringleader. They are the only people who had an interest in the paintings."

"Good grief. I mean, what a piece of work that is. Wait a minute. I remember that the director had to resign. That's right; it was in the papers years ago. Yeah, there was something faulty about that company. I can't believe that now," remembered Orry.

"I see. I suppose it would be listed somewhere. I will check. Thanks for the tip. The answer may have been right under our noses all this time," admitted Nicholas.

"That is right. The director Fabian Deburgh left under questionable circumstances."

"Deburgh. I think that it rings a bell. Actually, my cousin Imogen was married to a Deburgh."

"Well, you might want to check that out."

"Yes, I think that I will." Nicholas took a sip of his Martini.

"What are you having for lunch?"

"I think I'll have the crab and avocado to start. Nadia wants me to eat healthy."

"Sounds good. I think that I will try one of those."

The afternoon wore on as the two had a wonderful lunch, followed by panna cotta and bread pudding for dessert.

"You just can't beat the traditional desserts here," admitted Orry.

"Gosh, I remember the chocolate meringues. They don't do them here any more."

"I know. It is all changing. It is as if we have had our time, and there is always something new to take over."

"That is right. Changes are happening all the time. My life has changed. I never asked for it. It just changed."

"That's right, old chap. It just does."

The two finished with coffee and biscuits by 3 p.m. Nicolas enjoyed a refreshing summer walk back to the flat. The day was filled with nostalgia. He could almost hear Margaux as he walked through the door.

"Mildred, how are you?"

"Fine, Mr Mullbury. I was just in Knightsbridge overseeing the flat for Amy's arrival in the morning. I am so happy to have her back and to know that this mess will be dead and buried."

"That's right. Now try not to mention it to her. I would not want her to get upset. We want her to have a lovely summer like when she was little."

"That's right. I won't say a word. Marietta will have a lovely meal prepared, and then I am sure that they will go straight to bed."

"She always gets so jet-lagged. Try to keep an eye on things for a few days. We are just finalising everything with the lawyers. I Iank should have good news in a few days, and we wouldn't want to upset her. She has to get back into her normal routine."

"Right you are, Mr Mullbury. Right you are," replied Mildred. Mildred had been working for the family for decades and was a god-send after Margaux passed. She was trained by Margaux and knew her recipes and customs and could keep things going until Amelie got over the pain. Mildred had taken care of Amelie since she was a little girl and had never stopped. She was a rewarded and appreciated extended member of the family.

"Now have you seen Nadia?"

"Not yet. She has been working very hard on the performance. We shall have a rising star very soon."

"Yes indeed, and we will all have to support her on her big night.

Now I must get back to the den. I want to check to see if the flight is on time."

Nicholas recalled many transatlantic Friday evening flights back to home. He knew the route that Amelie would take from the house to the airport to the flat. It was always a smooth flight; he knew that there would be no issues. He was thankful for the life that he had helped to create, and his daughter's lifestyle was a part of it. She was not spoiled, just practical with what had been handed to her. He picked up the phone to call Hank to tell him what he had found out at lunch.

"The bank has been in shady dealings, and there was a director called Deburgh. I will have Mr Hoover check it out. Imogen was married to a Deburgh. I wonder if there is a connection."

"I see. Perhaps I can check on that, do a bit of investigating. And I will let Roger know. We are getting closer.

"We sure are. Amelie is coming in the morning. No more about the case until we get it sorted."

"All right, Dad. No more," agreed Hank.

Mildred continued in the kitchen and living room, setting the table for dinner. She had made some scallops and chips and had placed them in the microwave for Nadia's convenience when she arrived.

"Right, Mr Mullbury, I am through here. I have left the dinner in the microwave. It is still piping hot. If there isn't anything more, I think I will leave. I want to plan for Amy."

"Thank you for everything today. Yes, do please see to the flat in Knightsbridge. Have a lovely weekend."

"Thank you. I'll see you soon."

Managing the properties had been her main task for years. She was pleased to be a part of the family and worked endlessly for the Mullburys, sometimes sacrificing her own family time to do so.

"Darling, are you there?" asked Nadia as she returned after rehearsals.

"Yes. In the study, dear."

"Hello." She popped her head in.

"You are home early for a Friday." He checked his watch. It was just past seven.

"I know. I missed you, dear. We wrapped up early, and instead of drinks, I came straight home.

Pleased by her response, he answered, "Mildred has left the meal in the microwave."

"Fabulous. I will heat it up as soon as I change." She stood in her theatre leggings and sweater after a long rehearsal. He was becoming accustomed to the new look, but he preferred her lounge attire.

"See you, dear." Nicholas received two texts, one from Hank and the other from Amelie.

"We have sorted that horrible mess and will be signing the waiver agreement from Jude," wrote Hank. Nicholas requested a company search on Fabian Deburgh and Lynx in reply.

"We are at the airport, and the flight will leave at eight. See you soon. Love, A."

Nicholas was pleased to see both texts. Finally it was all ending and would be sorted by next week, in time to guarantee his daughter's safety. The company search should give more information, and then they could go to the authorities to give it a proper investigation. There would now be a whole host of people whom Amelie had never met before. It would take some getting used to for her. He would not impose it all on her as she would just be settling back into her routine.

Chapter 8

Welcome Home

Summer was bright, and there was a fresh breeze. The car drove up to the front door of 34 Beneville Road at about eleven. Amelie and Lars opened the cast-iron gates and dragged their luggage up the steps and into the foyer. Marietta heard the noise and ran to greet them as they arrived. She assisted with the luggage.

"It may seem as though they are a bit heavier. Nan has goodies for everyone."

Without fail she had traditional treats for her family that Verena had laboured over for hours.

"I see. Not to worry," replied Marietta, overly pleased to see them.

"That's great. It smells wonderful in here."

"Yes, I have just made some omelettes and muffins. I was not sure how hungry you would be."

"Thanks. I think we will have a quick bite and a nap after we have freshened up," suggested Lars.

"It will all be in the kitchen once you are ready."

"Great. We are going to head up and be down again soon," added Amelie.

They could not hide their fatigue. It had been a long flight, and it was still early in the morning for them. They clambered up the stairs and into their welcoming suite, where Amelie flopped on the bed and stared at the ceiling. The bedding was all fresh. She drew the fresh air from the open window which overlooked the back garden. The smell of summer and sweet flowers emanated the room. She truly felt grounded again.

"I am so relaxed. Let's just hang out for a while. I want to feel the warmth of home."

"Sure thing." Lars collapsed next to her and stretched out his hands. "I could nap right now."

"So could I."

They closed their eyes for what seemed like a few moments. When they awoke, Amelie glanced at the clock.

"My word. It is 2 p.m. We must have been knocked out."

"What, already?" Lars asked, arising from a deep slumber.

"Yes. Actually, we needed it."

"Must be. Do you think brunch is still downstairs? Let's have it up here."

"I think that it is a good idea."

"I'll go and bring it up to you."

"Thank you, darling. You do not have to," she said, pleased.

"Not to worry. Stay there. I will be right up."

Amelie looked at her messages. Nicholas had been texting to see if she was OK. She typed back, still a bit jet-lagged. He wanted to have lunch Sunday at the game. She wanted to check with Lars before answering as he had work piled up. She supposed that she could just go alone.

"Here we are then. Smoked salmon, eggs, and croissants. A bit of a late brunch."

"Thank you, darling. That smells good. And lovely coffee."

"Thought that we needed it."

"Certainly," she complied.

"Let's see what's on the news." He flipped through the channels.

"Are you free tomorrow? Dad wants to have lunch."

"No. I am in the office tomorrow. Sorry," he replied apologetically.

"Right then. I will just go. It would be good to see him after all this time."

"Yes. You just have a lovely lunch. I am really sorry, but I will have to pass. You know that there must be mountains of work."

"I know. Wishful thinking. I suppose that he wants to update me on the case. I do hope that it is all finalised."

"Yes. I do too." He tucked into his meal and sipped his coffee.

The sun shone brightly that Saturday afternoon in Knightsbridge. The streets were bustling as shoppers were preparing for the rest of the week. People sat at the outdoor cafes and basked in the protruding rays. There was a heat wave, and the city was energised.

Nicholas waited for Amelie at the restaurant in Mayfair. He had booked a table near the window. Nadia had rehearsal in the West End and would miss lunch. He wanted quality time with his daughter. She waltzed in, a bit flustered from the heat.

"Hello, dear. Welcome back. How have you been?"

"Hello, Dad. Lovely to see you. Jet-lagged."

"I see. Not to worry, dear. It will all be all right as usual."

"I know. It is only about 8 a.m. my time."

"Sure. I thought that you would like to hear the news."

"Yes, please. Do go on."

"Well. We have come along, and there is a Knot Linx and Fabian Deburgh from a private bank who seem to be behind it all. There never was a sale of the asset, but they had been in negotiations with your mother. I am so sorry, dear, to bring this up. We have been tipped off by Jude Deneuve. He will be in London in a few weeks to wrap this all up. We have the orders out against the gang members, and it seems now the authorities can deal with the ringleaders. I think that you are out of danger, dear."

"Thank God. This whole thing has gone on for too long. I can just get on with my life now, and things can be back to normal. I can't bear this any longer."

"I know. There are brighter roads ahead. Now, what do you want? I shall have the salmon filet. And you ...?"

"Just the eggs Benedict and salad. I need brunch now."

"Perfect. And to drink?"

"I think the smoothie to start. I need a pick-me-up," she replied.

"Sure thing. I think that I will have a Bloody Mary."

"Nan sends her love," she continued.

"How are they doing?"

"Very well. She is looking forward to seeing you."

"I know. It will be a lovely break once the production is finished. You will come and see it?"

"Of course. I would not miss it."

"Great. Nadia will be pleased."

"I know." Amelie did anything to appease them because her actions affected them incredibly.

"Lance is coming along, so you will get a chance to see him at last."

"Yes. At last." She was relieved that he had come through his operation.

"Also, you may get a chance to meet Mr Deneuve. He will be in London this month."

"I will see. I am not too sure I want to get too involved."

"It is entirely up to you. He has been rather cooperative. His family have known your family for such a long time. Their line goes back almost as long as yours. It would be a shame as he has been so helpful in this."

"Perhaps then. Perhaps." She did not want to commit to anything. She had so much to commit to already. "I have so much work to catch up on since I have been gone."

"Sure. You will get it all done, and you will get back into the swing of things. You'll see," he assured her.

"Well. I always do," she replied, convinced.

She always enjoyed her time with Nicholas. She felt safe and secure when he was around. They made memories at the restaurant every time they met. She felt that familiar bond that she always felt when she met him. The waiter brought the meal, and they enjoyed the rest of the afternoon talking over the enticing portions. It did not take her long to become reacquainted with her lifestyle. Nicholas always knew how to do just the trick. She left reinforced and optimistic. She felt as though this could work out for her and her summer could still be as hoped.

They walked for a few minutes before she got in the taxi. Another Sunday in Mayfair, and it had been a dream. She always thought of Margaux at the functions, what she would say and how she would say things back to her. She reminisced of old conversations as if they still were happening, thinking of what her mother might have said to make it all better. Now all water under the bridge for her. Amelie yearned for the chance to say the same and to do the same with her own child one day.

Once back at the house, she called her aunt. She needed to hear for herself that her uncle would pull through. She could not cope with any more bad news and needed to exert control over her life and surroundings. It had been out of sorts for too long.

"Hello, dear. It is lovely to hear from you."

"Thanks, Auntie. I had to call to know how you are all doing. I have missed you."

"We have missed you too. I am happy to say that Lance has made it through the tough part and is now convalescing well. We will have another consultation next week."

"That is wonderful news. I am so relieved. I have been so worried and just had to call you."

"I know. I know." Marguerite had been briefed by the family about the case and herself was looking forward to the end of the matter. It had dragged on for too long. She did not want to put too much strain on Amelie as she had been through so much the past few years.

"I can't wait to see you. I have so much to do workwise, and then we shall make a point to come up for a weekend."

"That would be lovely. Your uncle would be so pleased to see you. How was your trip?"

"Perfect. I am so lucky that my grandparents are holding on. I cannot wait to get back into my summer plans now."

"I know. Such a bother that you had to spend time away. This whole other mess will soon be over too."

"That is right. Dad thinks that they should wrap it up this week. Of course, he wants me to meet that Jude person."

"I see. His father knew my father. The two families go a long way back. They were like family until this whole thing started. We thought that it had been finalised years ago. Margaux and I had dealt with it after Father died. However, it has still come back to haunt us. Horrible mess that is. Acting as though we had sold things. That horrible bank and those culprits. They should all be in jail by now." Marguerite was adamant about her feelings. She thought that there had been too much disruption and undercutting of the issue, not to mention that the culprits had ruined Amy's life in the process. She had an inkling that she'd had been approached and wanted to protect her.

"I know. Should I meet him? It all sounds so strange and unconventional."

"Do as you wish. If you are appreciative of what he has done, then it would be diplomatic, as Father would say, to do your duty."

"I see. I will think about it some more. I never knew of this person and have no idea what he is like."

"I understand, dear. It is up to you." Marguerite knew the underlying story between the families. If Jude was anything like his father, then he would be attractive and also desirable. Her niece had to be warned. There was nothing like the handsome stranger to assist the damsel in distress. It seemed as though they had found too many damsels in their family. This meeting between Amelie and Jude was inevitable. They had protected her for such a long time. Her father was not acquainted with the draw of the Deneuve men.

"I need time for this one. I am just getting settled in," Amelie professed.

So much for a stress-free time, thought Marguerite. "I would not worry about it. You have other things right now. We are looking forward to seeing you in a few days."

"That is right. See you soon. Send my best to Uncle Lance."

"I will, dear. Talk soon. Bye now."

"Bye," she replied despondently.

Amelie was no more enlightened when she hung up. She had hoped that more light would have been shed. It was obvious that there was something about this relationship that made it all necessary. She would do her duty, that is all. It could do no harm meeting Jude with Hank and Nicholas. It would be pointless to drag Lars into something that would not be a constant in their lives, and besides, he might not understand why she would have to be a part of it all. Maybe he would. She would run it past him to get his reaction. She rung him at work.

"Hello, dear. Is something the matter?"

"No. Just wanted to see how you are doing?"

"Very busy, as you can tell. How was lunch with Nick?"

"We had a brilliant time. I am still a bit jet-lagged. How about you?"

"Just a bit, dear. Is something the matter?" he asked again.

"Dad has suggested that I meet this Jude, who will be arriving next week. What do you think?" she divulged.

"Well. That is a shock. I suppose it's all right," he replied, perplexed.

"OK then. I suppose I should," she responded.

"Well, only if you wish. Is there a problem?"

"No, no. I just needed your opinion, darling. That is all."

"Good. I will have to talk with you later. We are so much involved with work here."

"Thanks. Bye, dear."

"Bye."

Amelie had received her answer. She would meet Jude and then leave it at that. It was best that she not get too close anyway since she was uncertain of what was going on. Also, he would be under legal advice, and who knows what could come up!

She settled in and worked on the computer until she grew tired again and needed a nap. She was certainly worlds apart from where she had been the Friday before. Her trip now was a refreshing memory that she could recall during times like these. She had arranged the whole trip for Mr Mitchvale and would send him all his bookings and itinerary. It was already 6 p.m. and no sign of Lars. She supposed that he would have a late night at the office and she would have an early morning. She caught up on much-needed sleep.

When she awoke, Lars was beside her and in a deep slumber. She strained her eyes to look at the clock. It was close to midnight and nearly 7 p.m. her time. She was famished and wandered downstairs to find something. Marietta had left a few items in the fridge, but she just needed some fruit to snack on. She had not heard Lars come in, and he'd left her to sleep. *How considerate,* she thought. She had some pear and cheese and prepared for bed. She knew that it would take some time to get back to sleep. She might even be up most of the night now. Selfishly she thought that she should wake him. *No, let him sleep. He needs it after all that work,* she thought. She assembled her nightclothes and checked the latest news on her iPad. She could still make the tennis finals and the boating; however, she had missed most of the season and would have to contact Lorraine, Roger's wife, to see how it all went. She would wait until later, after the dreaded meeting with this new person.

The morning sun intruded into the room at about 5 a.m. Amelie had turned over to find that she had had only a few hours' sleep. She placed a mask over her eyes and tried to get back to sleep. She was in awe of how Lars had managed to sleep like a log this whole time and anticipated that he would arise soon. She'd hardly spoken to him about the dilemma, and she needed his input. She fell into a deep sleep and was out of sorts at 8 a.m.

"Rise and shine, darling. It is time for work," Lars teased with a cup of coffee.

"Brilliant. Thank you, dear. Lovely," she said as she took a sip.

"Now good luck today. I know that it is your first day back after a lovely few weeks on an enticing island."

She laughed. "Thank you, dear. Same to you." She inspected him and saw that he was dressed and ready to go.

"Thank you. I must be off."

"Bye, dear. What time did you get in last night? I did not hear you come in."

"I think that it must have been about ten. You were out like a light. I did not want to disturb you, dear."

"I see. When I awoke, you were still asleep. I did not want to disturb you, dear," she mimicked.

"Good. I will see you later. Call me at work."

"Sure. I will."

"Have a lovely day," he encouraged her.

"I will. Just as soon as I get ready," she joked.

She remembered how much of a joy that it was to get ready, especially for a lovely summer's day. She filed through her lovely summer dresses and chose a patterned one in cream and sea foam along with a cream blazer and some patent leather beige pumps. She whisked her hair into a bun and applied cover-up and a frosty pink blush with pink lip gloss. It was all so fresh and summery. It would be a sweltering day. The car was ready to take her to the office. Delianna was there bright and early and excited to see her.

Amelie waltzed in, ecstatic to be back and overly animated when greeting the staff.

"Welcome back. We have missed you," Delianna exclaimed.

"Thank you. It is lovely to be back. And what a lovely day," replied Amelie.

"It will be like this all week. We have been hoping for this day," admitted Delianna.

"Thanks. You have done a superb job in my absence. You all have," she said, turning to the other two, who were seated within ear's distance. They were attentive in her presence and gave bright smiles as she glanced at them.

"How have you been?"

"Fine, just fine." Teddy nodded.

"Fine, very well," replied Melanie, nodding.

"Perfect. It is lovely to be back. And now to the desk." Amelie headed to her office, where she could see her in tray had piled up and some personal letters had been left on the desk. Delianna followed her in.

"Well, these are just for you to sort through. I have been through the post, but these looked personal, so I left them to one side. You have a conference call with a new client, Mrs Somerville, at 3 p.m. Of course I tried to clear your in tray a bit, but I am sure that you have seen most of it."

"Thank you. You have done a wonderful job keeping this all in order. Can you tell me more about Mrs Somerville?"

"Yes. Recently divorced and needs a three-month plan for the rest of the summer. Wants to travel the world; her children are away, and she is a bit lonely. Mind you, she did receive a very good settlement and wants to travel the Serengeti and Melbourne."

"Right then. I will do some prepping. It is a bit out of the ordinary for us—I mean the safari—but we can handle it. I have just the place."

"I knew that you would. Also, a new client needs help with a trip down under this summer."

"Great. Will get on that as well. Thank you." Amelie dismissed Delianna, feeling a bit overwhelmed already on her first day back. She wished that had she known about the appointment today; she could have planned yesterday. She must have skipped over that email. She sorted through the mail, which was mostly to do with corporate responsibility, and went through her in tray. The euphoria of being back had ended, and now it was down to work. She had to plan a catered journey to Kenya and Australia.

She had lunch at her desk. Teddy had brought back sushi for them all. She had given him the task of researching Melbourne, while she researched Kenya. It was a beautiful place. She had always wanted to go herself. She imagined herself some sort of "West by Night" figure who could take on the world doing good for others in an exotic location. Perhaps one day she could. The corporate objective of helping others start up in business could do quite well in Kenya, she thought. She was already a supporter of several charities, and she could move to that.

She stopped herself from being distracted and researched the safari. It was beautiful, and the sunset was enticing. She could really do this. Teddy returned with the information on Melbourne. It all looked so enticing, the large hotel and all the activities. This was really a client on a soul-searching mission. She had to plan this one right and with the right security.

"It is lovely to talk to you. We are pleased to be taking you on. I just need to know a little about your objective and what to expect from this journey?" asked Amelie.

"Well. It has been a difficult two years of legal battle, and we have just finalised the divorce. My children are on gap years and soon off to college, and I want to live a little, but in the catered sense since I am embarking on my own. I have always read about the Serengeti and have wanted to visit. I love that film, you know, the one about the author and the farm in Africa. Perhaps I can find my leading man. I also need a trip to Australia. I want to experience the wonderful Outback. I knew that you could help."

"Sure. It will be our pleasure. This is catered and sustainable. We will have you looked after from door to door. So we will package everything so that you will have nothing to worry about."

"Thank you. I have had deals before, and sometimes places do not acknowledge certain vouchers when they are foreign."

"Not to worry. I personally contact the vendors and have an access code. Trust me. They will see the money beforehand for this to work. And I only use reputable people who will honour our transactions. You have a hotline for the office for any emergencies, and you will see that I only deal with reputable partners."

"Well, that is a relief. Because you never really know once you leave."

"Exactly. That is why I am glad that you came to us."

"Perfect. Now I am thinking of travelling from August to October, and I can spend about thirty thousand pounds."

"That will do, I am sure. Of course. Most will be on the travel and the hotels."

"I am not particular. I can go business or premium. I just want the proper service at the locations."

"That sounds good. Then there will be more for trip security. We will put together several packages for you to choose from, and then you can get back to us with your preferences."

"Sounds good. I will talk to you soon."

"Thank you for choosing us." Amelie hung up. She knew that it would be a task. At least she had a good budget to work with, even though the commission would be minimal as she would have to outsource a lot of the services.

"Right. Teddy, we need a plan for this. I will contact a few numbers in Melbourne and Kenya to get some quotes. This is all a bit exciting," she confessed.

"Yes. Sure, I will get right on it," he replied professionally.

He left. It was almost teatime. Amelie needed a coffee break. This would take all night. It would soon be morning abroad, and she was jet-lagged.

Hank and Nicholas entertained Jude at the table while they waited for Amelie to arrive.

"I am glad that we cracked this case and finally we can move on. It has been dreadful for Amelie," Hank advised.

"It is my intention to be helpful. I have been suspicious since it happened. I think there was an attempt to warn you," Jude admitted.

"Really? When was that?" enquired Nicholas.

"It was about a year ago. However, the chance was missed because it was too sensitive. No one expected that what happened would have happened. It had been dormant for so long. It was a surprise to me," admitted Jude.

"I see. Well, we will get those directors, and they will talk. Good work on your part."

"Thank you. It was the least that I could do. The families have been close all my life, and my father and grandfather always spoke so highly of you all. Admittedly they were disappointed by Lou and Margaux's decision about the sale. However, I understand perfectly."

"That is a relief. Now Amelie has had a tough time, so let us keep the conversation a bit light when you meet her. We would not want to worry her," advised Hank.

Amelie rushed in, aware of the time and looking at her watch. She was wearing a green silk scarf and navy linen suit with a cream blouse.

"Sorry that I am late. Dad, Hank." She nodded.

"Not to worry. Perfect timing," answered Nick.

"Wonderful." She took a seat next to Hank and across from Jude and Nick.

"Now. We have just been chatting about the old days, dear. This is Jude, an old friend of the family."

"I am pleased to meet you." She extended her hand.

"Enchanté, Madame. We finally meet after all these years," replied Jude.

"The pleasure is mine, I am sure," she responded cautiously.

"Well. Would you like a menu?" interrupted Hank.

"Certainly. It would be lovely to see what the summer menu is like. We always come here," she explained to Jude.

"I see. It is a lovely place. Lovely ambiance. And it is a perfect day," noted Jude.

"What a relief. Such a lovely day. And I am finally back home," she replied.

"Yes. Welcome back, old girl. What can we get you?" asked Hank.

"Just a Prosecco, and I will have a look at the menu. My, the scallops look good."

"Well, Prosecco it is," answered Hank as he motioned to the waiter.

"Thank you."

"How is work going?" asked Nick.

"We have two new clients, and I am just settling back into the swing of things. Hopefully some tennis next week."

"That sounds interesting," responded Jude. "I have not been to Wimbledon since my father was alive. He loved to come here. Such a pity that we have not met before. I think that the transaction ruined everything. Here is to new ties and old friends," he toasted as her drink arrived.

"Hear! Hear!" Nicholas and Hank raised their glasses, while Amelie obliged.

"Well, you are welcome to join us. I am sure that we can find an extra place with the concierge," she offered.

"Would you? That would be fantastic. I would look forward to extending my trip to go down memory lane," he said.

He was sincere. He was with old friends who needed a hand. His eyes had a very meaningful expression and were sunken in their sockets when he was distressed. They were like turquoise pools that were the windows to his soul. His sensitivity was on display. Amelie noticed it.

"It would be my pleasure. Thank you for helping us. We really appreciate it."

"It is the least that I could do. When Mr Hoover arrived, I realised how serious things were. I would not want to see any harm come to any of you. Things took a turn for the worse, and I am very sorry."

"Not to worry. It is all sorted now," expressed Nicholas, pleased at Amelie's hospitality.

"Shall we order?" asked Hank.

"Yes. Let's," responded Nicholas.

They chatted over dinner about the old days and the summers they spent on the Continent. It seemed as though Jude's life was similar to Amelie's. They had holidayed in the same places and had travelled often to similar places. He had to take over the business and manage the family estate until he sold it to live in Switzerland. They spoke of stories that Amelie had never heard before. She grew more receptive towards him and realised that he was just like one of them. She was pleased to have seen him after all. It was another tie to her mother, one that opened onto a new world that she had never known.

The meals were light and delicious. They ended the afternoon with French desserts and wine.

"I will see you again, Hank, at the lawyer's office."

"Yes, that is right. Bright and early tomorrow."

"Well, thank you for having lunch with us," added Amelie.

"The pleasure was mine. Until we meet again," Jude replied.

"Yes. I will get back to you regarding the tennis."

"Please do. That would be lovely."

"Bye, Dad. Hank."

"Bye, dear. Thank you." Nicholas was pleased that everything had gone well.

"Bye, Amy. Will chat soon," replied Hank. He was a bit irked by it all, the way that Jude ingratiated himself with Amelie and the way she had obliged. He sensed that there was more to it and wondered what Jude wanted. He would find out. Perhaps it was a bit more than mutual admiration. There were stories about Margaux and Clyde before she'd met Nicholas. Did he have a family obligation to prove something? The answers were yet to be seen in his perspective.

Amelie returned to work and continued her planning for her clients to Africa and Australia. When she was burrowed in her work, she was most satisfied. She did not want to think of the horrors and the evil people in her life. This had gone on for too long and was not meant to get in the way of her happiness.

The phone rang. It was her husband. "Darling, I so happy to hear from you," she patronised.

"Just checking in to see how it all went?"

"It went rather well. Quite a nice person. You get to meet him next week."

"I do? Why is that?" he asked, perturbed.

"I asked him to the tennis match next week. Is that OK? We can invite someone else along to keep him company. I think that it is a good idea for us four," she explained.

"Sure. I mean, wouldn't it be strange, seeing that he is in on the case, to be at such a high-profile event?"

"I did not think about that. I don't think it would make a difference. Issues are in the clear, right?"

"Sure. That is right. Look, there is nothing wrong with it from a personal point of view," he concluded.

"Yes. Precisely. You will see that it will work out fine. He is a nice guy," she reasoned.

"Fantastic. We had better find out if we can get a place at the table."

"Sure. I will do that."

Amelie hung up, a bit confused by Lars's response. Had she overstepped the mark from a legal perspective? She had no idea and did not have the time to ponder. It could not be such a big deal anyway. She ensconced herself in her work. It was too much to bother about pleasing everyone and being diplomatic after what she had been through. Besides, Jude had so much history, and in that history was her mother.

It was already later in the time zones of her targeted destinations. She concentrated on her uncle and his welfare. They were planning to spend time in Surrey at Vicomte Manor. His prognosis was good, and he was almost in the clear. Amelie also would speak to Marguerite about the Deneuve family. If there was anyone who would know about them, it was her.

Nicholas arrived back at the flat in Mayfair, relieved that they had cracked the case. The authorities were investigating the fraud of the DeSabulus Bank, the directors, and the sale, and the bank's and the directors' involvement with Mesnel and Shadrock, who were facing obstruction charges. The future looked brighter. The Mullburys had also become reacquainted with an old family friend. It had brought him a sense of déjà vu. He found that the summer also brought back memories of his past life with Margaux. It was not too far from the time of year when Lou and Margaux threw parties on Park Lane. He remembered her summer cologne, tea rose and gardenia. She wore it every summer with patterned lounge dresses, bejewelled sandals, and floppy hats. He remembered the meringues and dessert wines and the concerts in Hyde Park. He went down to the study and rummaged through that old file again.

He knew that he was the centre of her life. However, he was uneasy about her relationship with Clyde Deneuve. The close family friendship was paramount, but was it masking a bit more underlying? Would she have been honest with him? What was the purpose of dragging the past out now? Why was he so entitled to those assets? Were there past promises between them that were unrequited? Margaux loved her family dearly, of that he was certain, but he was feeling some doubt because of the walk down memory lane.

He found a letter to Clyde. He read it over and over, looking for clues. He understood the diplomacy of it; however, he read between the lines and deciphered all that it did not say. Why had Margaux been so understanding with people who had been hounding her to sell? Why did she walk away and not dig deeper to ensure that they would never have the possibility of owning the assets? He needed more answers and was afraid to ask Marguerite, Margaux's closest confidant, who would have them. She had so much to worry about with Lance, so he decided to wait a bit longer, as there was no rush after all these years.

Nadia walked in, and his spirits lifted. His life was with her whether he could accept it fully or not, and he had to move on.

"Hello, darling. What are you reading? You look deep in thought."

"Nothing, dear. Just some old correspondence." He brushed it off.

"I see. You have been a bit distracted recently. Is everything OK?"

"Yes. Fine, dear. Just mulling over a few things from the case."

"I wish that it would end. You have been so preoccupied since this started up again. Can I do anything to cheer you up?"

"Why don't we have a quiet night in with some wine?"

"Sounds lovely. Just what I was thinking for this humid summer evening. It is much cooler indoors than it is outdoors."

"Perfect. Leave it up to me."

She left, satisfied, and climbed the stairs to get ready. He could only be certain about the present and had to bury the past.

Amelie and Lars drove to Surrey and entered the parking lot of Vicomte Manor. He parked the Land Rover at the edge of the circular driveway, and they disembarked. Amelie carried a basket of treats from the bakery in South Kensington.

She hugged Marguerite as she entered and could see that the events of the past month had affected her. She was bewildered from the ordeal and fatigued by the emotional roller coaster.

"How are you doing?" asked Amelie.

"Fine, dear. Just fine. Your uncle is stable and much better. They say that he will make it."

"Good news. Fantastic."

"Hello, Aunt Marguerite. Lovely to see you as usual," added Lars.

"The same to you. I hope that you had a lovely stay at Winifred's."

"Yes. Perfect. But we could not wait to return after awhile. We stayed so long that we missed part of this season."

"I know. You will make it up. It has not been the ideal summer so far."

"I still have not gotten over it. However, we have the tennis next week, and we are taking Clyde with us."

"Really?" She looked at them both, perplexed.

"Apparently he is here for another week and did not have much planned. It was the right thing to do, wouldn't you say?" she asked Lars.

"Yes. Fine. I get to meet this infamous character who has been the saving grace of it all," replied Lars, chivalric.

"I see. I have not seen him since he was little. He was such an ideal little boy. He looked just like his father."

"Really. I do not remember the family much. Just the odd conversation. It is amazing how life works out. I guess what is meant to be will be," reasoned Amelie.

"I suppose, dear. Now let us see your uncle. He has been waiting all morning to see you."

"Great."

When they entered the sitting room, they saw Lance sitting with a light blanket on his lap and the windows open to circulate the air.

"Is that you, my dear niece?" he asked jovially.

"Yes, Uncle, it's us. We have been so concerned and are overjoyed that you are doing better."

"Yes. I have come almost full circle since the operation. It has been a month, and the prognosis is positive."

"I know. We have been really hoping and praying." She looked at Lars, who agreed.

"Have a seat. Let me look at you," he ordered.

She complied, grateful that she could treasure this moment that now exists. She had been so worried over the last few weeks that she cherished every moment.

"I can't wait until the holiday at the chateau later this summer," she continued.

"Yes," he agreed. "Should be like the others."

"Gosh, I have such memories of things over the years. Don't I?" she looked at Lars, who sat next to her.

"Yes. You do. So do I," he added.

Lance became amused by his reverie. "Would you like a drink? Bourbon, sherry, wine? We shall have lunch soon."

"Sure. That would be lovely."

"Which one?" asked Lance.

"Bourbon for me," answered Lars.

"Well, wine for me, thanks," responded Amelie.

Marguerite was in the kitchen with the helper, finalising the mint soup for the appetiser. She had made a leg of lamb with new potatoes and a summer fruit pudding with heavy cream. Lars enjoyed these visits as it gave him an excuse for a large meal, although he was on strict diet and would not have everything on the menu. He would skip the bread, the cheese, and the cream and have sparkling water as a refreshment to drink instead.

"Lunch is served," announced Marguerite as she entered to collect them and move them to the dining room. It was all immaculately set with lace tablecloths and mats, fine bone china, and crystal goblets. Amelie could remember the settings as traditional and loved the smooth silverware.

"I just love this setting," complimented Amelie.

"Yes. It is the usual for a Saturday afternoon lunch," responded Marguerite as she sat. The assistant passed the bowls of soup. "The mint is fresh from the garden," she said proudly.

"It is delicious," added Amelie with the example of good manners.

"Yes, lovely. This is my favourite," added Lars.

"Fabulous, darling, as always," added Lance.

"Thank you, darlings."

Amelie could smell the garlic and parsley of the new potatoes and parsnips just then roasting. The next course would be delightful.

"We appreciate the time that it took. You always make such a good meal. I can't wait for the next course."

Marguerite was pleased by her etiquette. She was always so appreciative of the little things, and she could not have asked for a better niece. The afternoon passed quickly. The sun peaked at about 3 p.m., and it was sweltering out. It had been an unusually hot summer, and the grounds were not as plush as usual. The view of the garden was vast and continued way beyond the glass doors. Amelie left reassured that she would not be saying her final goodbyes at that time. She was relieved.

Chapter 9

Sporting Days

The weather could not have been better for the men's tennis finals. Amelie put on her classic white sleeveless dress, and Lars his classic blue blazer and cream brimmed hat, and the two were ready for the games to begin. They drove to the hospitality area to meet their new guest. Amelie had asked along Karen from her previous office because she was recently single.

"I assume that they are here by now. It is time for the lunch," Amelie commented as Lars parked the car.

"I suppose," answered Lars unassumingly. It would be a testy day for him. He was embarking on unchartered waters and had yet to know the outcome. They wandered into the pavilion, where Amelie could see that Jude was sipping a cocktail at the bar.

"Here he is. I want you to meet him," she continued as she led the way to the bar. Jude turned just in time and saw them.

"Hello, hello," he greeted her.

"Wonderful to see you. Have you been waiting long?"

"No, not at all."

"This is my husband, Lars."

"It is my pleasure. I appreciate having the chance to come along today," Jude answered.

"Well, it is great to have you. Glad that you could make it. I am sure that you will enjoy the tennis," Lars commented.

"I hope so. It has been awhile for me. I have had not had the chance to enjoy the British summer since my father passed away."

"Oh, dear. I am sorry to hear that. We will make it up today," empathised Lars.

"Yes. It will be great fun. And the food is fantastic here."

"That's right, always a good time. Can I offer you another drink before we are seated?"

"Sure. I will have another, thank you," replied Jude obligingly.

"There she is," commented Amelie as she waved to Karen.

"Hello, hello. I am sorry I am a bit late. The bus was stuck in traffic."

"Not to worry. So lovely to have you. This is Jude, an old family friend."

Karen seemed perplexed by his looks. "It is great to meet you," she stated.

"My pleasure. Enchanté," he returned with a peck on the cheek.

"I am sure," she said. Turning to Lars, she added, "Great to see you. It has been some time."

"That's right, not since the holidays."

"I know it does seem like a long time doesn't it?"

"Yes. We have so much to catch up on," replied Karen.

"Would you like a drink?" asked Lars.

"Yes, please. Some champagne."

"Great. Darling, what about you?"

"Some champagne. Why not? We are celebrating."

"That is right. It is a milestone for me," added Jude.

"Really? Why is that?"

"I have not been in years. Actually, it has been some time since I have been in the UK," he explained.

"Really? Why is that?"

"I have been busy with work in Geneva, and I have not found the time since my father passed."

"I am so sorry," she continued. "We will make it a point to make it special."

"That is right. Now shall we find our table. We will miss the start if we delay any more."

"Sure. Here is your champagne," said Lars.

"Shall we?" Amelie led the party to their table and assessed where everyone would be seated.

"Lars, please sit next to Karen, and I will sit here." She sat next to Jude and opposite Karen.

"This all looks so lovely."

"Yes. They really give you your money's worth here. Lars and I have so been looking forward to this. I missed so many events in June while in Bermuda."

"I know. Such a pity," responded Karen.

Lars changed the subject. "So, Jude, how much longer will you be with us?"

"Another week perhaps, and then back to the office. There is so much to do."

"I see. Although during the summer there must be a lull on the Continent. It appears to be a time when everyone is on holiday."

"Yes. That is right. Although perhaps more in August."

"I see. Well, it will be the right time to meet someone. These things usually happen when you have time on your hands."

"Hopefully. I must admit it has been a long time since I last dated."

"Really? Why is that?" asked Amelie.

"Well, I had so much responsibility when I took over the company, and my workdays just got longer and longer."

"I see. It can happen. Lars and I always had each other since university, so I really do not know what that is like," she admitted.

"That is a bit like me, though. Since my last break-up, I have been in the office working later and later it seems," added Karen.

"That is probably why we have not seen you. You have been bogged down in your work," joked Lars.

"I know. I must confess." She laughed.

The waitress took their orders.

"I do hope that I made the right choice. I did not have the time to really think it over. I usually get the seafood platter; however, I chose the risotto. A bit vegetarian. Look how superb the desserts are, though."

"I know. I think that there will be double time at the gym," commented Lars.

"I think that the chocolate mousse cake looks divine," answered Karen.

"Yes, it is a splendid menu. And I have heard that this is one of the best chefs in the country," added Jude.

"Absolutely. It was booked solid months ago," agreed Amelie.

"I am grateful to be a part of it," Jude responded appreciatively.

"It is our pleasure having you."

Lars grew uncomfortable with how his wife and Jude were so affable and were growing closer. He was concerned about the case; however, there was a tinge of something else that he had not felt in a long time. Was he jealous of their new-found friendship? He tried to reason that they were family friends and deserved this connection after the rift that they had experienced over the paintings. He could not put his finger on it, though. They looked so suitable for each other. Jude could be seen as a golden-boy type as Lars's Amy was always his golden girl. Lars was a bit in it over his head. He was not used to this type of competition for her attention. He decided to attempt to cast these insecurities aside and enjoy the afternoon.

Jude relished in the new friendship. He was comfortable around Amelie and had developed a sense of trust that was evident by their complacency at the table. Karen reacted as if she were talking to a group of old friends who had known each other for a very long time. Jude had slotted in to the family like no other. One might even think that he and Amelie were closer than they had let on and had known each other a bit longer.

The entrées were brought to the table, and the group tucked into their meals. After the champagne, they welcomed the nourishment and sipped sparkling water as the sun was starting to rise to its highest point.

"How is your meal?" Amelie asked the group.

"Lovely. I have made the right choice as usual," assured Karen.

"The platter is perfect," answered Jude.

"I am fine here," answered Lars. "And you, dear?"

"Fine, thanks."

"Perfect," he responded.

"Yes. It is not too heavy, so with a bit of coffee we will have an active afternoon watching the match," added Jude.

"That is right. There is afternoon tea at about 5 p.m. and then more matches. So I would not want to overdo it," cautioned Amelie.

"I think that I can remember. Now that is a feast," commented Jude.

"I know. It will be, so you had better save some room," added Lars.

"Well, we had better get a move on, or else we will miss the beginning of the match. I hate when that happens. And that is what we are here for," reminded Karen.

"That is right. You want to get to your seat and not wait around."

"Fine. Let's move on," added Lars.

After dessert, the group took the shuttle to the courts, where they were seated with a good view of the match. Again, Karen and Amelie sat next to Jude and tried to entertain him a bit before the match started. Lars started to check his phone for lunchtime messages. He knew that his inbox would be overflowing. They could hear silence as the balls landed across the court and were returned with the utter determination of the opponent. The volley would go on until finally one player would give in ultimately, which was no easy task. They fought to the finish like competitors do.

Lars felt uneasy watching and thought it strange that the match may just well be on the spectators' side. However, he was grateful for Jude's assistance in the case and for finally bringing the matter to rest. The case was developing and would soon be final thanks to his evidence.

Hank called Nicholas to fill him in on the developments.

"Hello. We have just finished the meeting with the authorities, and it seems as though the end is in sight."

"That is just the news that I have been waiting for. What exactly did they propose?"

"They have enough evidence to go after the directors for fraud and will be doing so in imminently. Also, the two culprits will be charged with obstruction, and the paintings will be restored fully to Mother's estate. The Deneuves receive concessions for their assistance, and now it is more than an attempted heist. It us a corporate fraud case where investors were conned. From this end, we have no more to do with it."

"What a relief. Amy will be pleased. And now Jude can head back, having accomplished what he set out to achieve. Such a pity that it did not all come to a revelation sooner."

"I know. It would have saved us so much trouble. To think that Mesnel and Shadrock were in jail all that time and did not want to assist with the enquiries. Hopefully we will never see the likes of them again."

"That's right. Never again. Roger is finalising the paperwork, and we have done our part with our wealth restored."

"I had no idea that it was in jeopardy. I think that it is better, of course, behind us. It still leaves the question of what to do with the painting now that it is all cleared," commented Nick.

"We will have to discuss that with Amy. She is busy at the tennis now, and Jude is there," he responded despondently.

"Well, now that it is all wrapped up, it should not do any harm. He will soon be gone, and she will get back into the swing of things like her business and the rest of the summer season."

"I know. Sooner rather than later. There is something about his arrogance," noted Hank.

"I think that all of them are like that. I really had a time with it all myself, so I can really sympathise with Lars. There is an entitlement that seems to go back a long way," he confided.

"Well. Whatever it is, it worked out, and it is over."

"Let us hope," commented Nicholas.

"When are you down to Nan's and Grandpapa's?"

"Next week. Not for a long break, as Nadia is working on the musical and has lots of rehearsals."

"I see. Will talk to you before then," replied Hank.

"Fabulous. Until then." Nicholas hung up, relieved. He also felt validated that Hank had the same trepidation that he himself had about the newly refound friend. He would take it all at face value and remember the family characteristics.

"You did not have to be so wary. He was only being affable," explained Amelie on the ride back to SW3.

"Really. I was quite pleasant. He has done so much, and I truly appreciate it."

"I see. I suppose that is why you asked about his love life. It is none of our business."

"Well, hang on. We were trying to find the right fit for Karen."

"I am sure that Karen can make up her own mind. She was right there and would have asked herself," explained Amelie.

"Really? I did not hear her ask. She was smitten, but he seemed to be a bit distracted."

"How can you say that after all that he has done? He was just reminiscing about old times, that is all. I am one of the only people he knows in this town."

"I see. Why is that? You would think that after a week, a man in his position would have found someone," observed Lars.

"I cannot be certain. He did explain about work," replied Amy.

"You are answering for him now?"

"Not really. I am a family friend, and we were on an outing, that is all."

"Yes. You invited him."

"Yes, as well as Karen. And we have had other friends over the years."

"He is like the others then?"

"Yes. I will consider him a friend now that he has shown his true friendship and is closing this case," she replied.

"Fantastic. The knight in shining armour and family friend."

"What is it? He will be gone soon. He is a family friend. They have known my family for generations. I am sorry."

"No need to apologise. I understand completely. It is all fine. Nothing more."

"Good. Nothing more."

The drive was awkward after the conversation. Lars let it all go and hoped that it was just passing phase.

Amelie could not understand what had overcome him. Was it jealousy or something else? Whatever it was, she did not have the time to ponder. The case had taken so much time, and it was now over. The proper summer could begin.

Lars broke the ice: "I hope that it will be brilliant weather for the regatta."

"So do I. We always enjoy that," she obliged.

"Yes, we always do. There are also the races."

"I know. Now that you do enjoy. We should invite Roger. Hopefully it will all be over by August."

"Hopefully."

"Then we have the South of France. A superb way to tie up the summer, don't you think?"

"That is when it is the hardest. Coming back from the August break to a bleak September and October."

"Not this time. We shall take a break and go to the country. It shall be the last of the summer wine. And we can ride on Polka and Velvet all over the estate."

"Can't wait, dear. I can't wait."

SW3 was in sight as they turned off the Brompton road and went back towards Knightsbridge. The energy boosted as they emerged in the centre of town and parked in front of their Edwardian home. Amelie got out and opened the iron gates to her doorstep. Stepping on the black and white tiles, she opened the door. She was back to her lovely home and the life she had created in it.

Jude arrived at the hotel on Hyde Park fully satisfied by the day's events. He was full of the optimism of having made the right choice and bringing the culprits to justice once and for all. He checked his phone and had a message from his attorney in Switzerland. He called instantly.

"Yes. It is all done now, and the waiver has been signed. There will be nothing else required on your end."

"Fabulous news. And Mr Gouter?"

"Yes, we have sorted him as well. He will not be implicated in that scheme to steal the paintings. They have been secured in ownership to the family, and the bank cannot claim any more ownership. The directors' work has been in vain, and the bank, and hopefully Linx and Deburgh, will be penalised for the fraud, wherever they may be, or the bank for that matter."

"Fantastic. I can return to Lausanne and get back to the business."

"Sure. The sooner, the better. You never know what else can arise."

"That is right. I will book my flight for tomorrow. I will make my excuses and leave."

"Bon soir."

"Bon soir." Jude hung up, elated. It had not been a wasted journey. He flicked through his camera at the photos of the day. Amelie's face was bright and cheerful. He knew that there would be something that he would miss, the closest chance that he had to a sister. To him she was so endearing and accommodating. She was understanding like a sister should be. If only there were more time to get to know her. He could always keep in touch from home and would call her from the airport to say goodbye. It would be better that way. He decided to inform Hank of his departure and make amends with her later. She would understand. Indeed, she seemed like the type of person who would actually miss him. Maybe he was reading too much into it. She was married after all. He thought, *Au revoir, ma cherie.*

Amelie checked her emails when she got back and found some from Delianna regarding Mr Mitchvale. He was planning another trip to New York and needed mobilisation. Also, her client Mrs Somerville had a very smooth flight to Kenya and was about to embark on her excursions in the Serengeti. It was all working out well.

Amelie knew that the end-of-summer trip to France was important for her and Lars—and also a real deal-breaker after all that they had been through in their marriage. It seemed as though things were a bit on ice. A lovely trip would be just the thing. She would also be able to check on the paintings at the museum and marvel at her family's art amid the French countryside in Bordeaux. She had idyllic visions of her and Lars on cycles and with knapsacks, riding through the quaint villages and stopping to see sights like when they were at university and exploring new territory.

It was just a memory. Their lives were so sophisticated now. If she could take it back to that point when they first fell in love, it would iron out any glitches from this whole ordeal. He had been her protector, and she still needed him and was so grateful.

Chapter 10

Theatre Nights

Nicholas called to tell Amelie the good news. "There is finally a break in the case, and it is all behind you, Amelie. You should be delighted. Now you can get on with your life."

"Finally. That is brilliant," she said ecstatically at the thought of a balanced life.

"I know. And we can thank Roger and Jude for their efforts. The paintings are secure in the family name, and there can't be any more fraud. I do hope that you can put this all behind you."

"Absolutely. I am busy with the planning of the holiday with Lars, and then I have some clients for whom I am planning trips to New York and Melbourne."

"Fabulous news. I am sure that they will be very pleased with whatever you are planning. Now you do remember that Nadia is having her production this weekend. You know it is a bank holiday, and then we all break for the summer. I am visiting Mum and Dad, and you will be going off yourself. It is important that we slot this in."

"Fine, Dad. Thanks for reminding me. I would be honoured to

attend. I know how hard she has been working. It will be a lovely outing for us."

"Great. There will be post theatre dinner for us to celebrate."

"Sounds perfect. See you this weekend."

"Bye. See you, dear."

Amelie got back to work. Mrs Somerville was embarking on her journey through the Serengeti and had two more weeks before heading to Melbourne, where a luxurious holiday awaited her. Mr Mitchvale was off to New York and needed plans to set him up on a two-week business trip. Amelie thought that a penthouse suite in the heart of the city would be ideal. She searched through her contacts for her property manager in New York. The sky was the limit for Mr Mitchvale; no luxury would be spared. Amelie hired everyone from the chauffer straight to the butler service. Mr Mitchvale was in the process of merging with a publishing company and needed everything at his disposal for those long business days at the negotiating table.

Amelie then turned her attention to her trip to France. She wanted to revisit a few areas where she and Lars had enjoyed their budding romance. A tour through Bordeaux or the Loire would be ideal, she thought. A few days in the old chateaux and the museums as well as the vineyards would do them some good and put this whole mess behind them. She would pass it by him to see what he had to say.

He arrived home that evening very distracted. "Have we any coffee?" he asked as he changed into his polo shirt and khakis.

"Sure, there should be some in the machine or in the pantry."

"I have a new case and need to get back to Malta. Probably next week."

"What? No, we were going to the regatta."

"I know, but I am sorry. Perhaps Lydia or Lorraine will go. I just can't. This has just come up again."

"Fine. I will try to find someone else. We always go."

"Sorry, dear. I am still catching up from the trip last month. We were gone an exceptionally long time."

"Not to worry. I understand," she replied despondently.

"Would you like the coffee?"

"I will get it. I know where it is."

"Perfect. Shall we order in tonight? Marietta had the afternoon off. Or I can make something."

"No. I can fry us up some omelettes or veggie stir-fry," he offered, remembering her diet.

"Sure. Sounds wonderful, Mr Chef. I'll look forward to it."

"Right. I will get to it. Have we any rice or quinoa?"

"Should be in the pantry. And the veggies should be in the fridge as Marietta just did the shopping."

"Fabulous."

Nicholas looked around nervously until he saw Amelie and Lars arrive at the theatre. Hank and Jenny were seated in the front row.

"Ah. Here you are. What a relief. The show is about to begin."

"Hello. Sorry that we are late. There was so much traffic on the road tonight."

"Usually at weekends, dear," he explained.

"Sorry. We are looking forward to the show," added Lars.

"Splendid. Shall we?" Nicholas asked as he showed the tickets to the usher.

"Sure. Do we want anything before?" asked Amelie.

"I think we can get something at the intermission. And we are having dinner later."

"Great. Let's go in then," she conceded.

"Perfect," Lars added.

They were ushered down the aisle to their seats, where Hank and Jenny awaited them.

"Hey, Sis. Glad that you could make it." He smirked.

"Traffic was horrible coming in," she said, making excuses.

"I know," he said apologetically.

They manoeuvred through the seating. Nicholas awaited the curtain rise like a child ready for a recital. It was important to Nadia that he show support.

Backstage she was nervous. She sat in her dressing room and applied her lipstick. Beside her was a bouquet of flowers from the family. She didn't know what she would have done without their support. She had been with Nicholas for four years and had not been on the stage for almost ten. She was filled with nerves and anticipation. It was opening night, and the reviewers were out like sharks.

"Nay, are you ready?" asked the producer.

"Certainly." She checked herself one last time in the mirror. She was dressed like a factory worker in the 1930s and fell into the Midland vernacular for her part. She flowed in on Act I, joined by her co-worker as her character lamented the tough times and her Johnny not being able to find work. Her diction was clear, and her voice could be heard through to the back of the theatre. Her cues were in sight, and she looked directly to the back, where the audience could see her. She had not lost her talent. She commanded the stage and drew the attention of the onlookers. The cast sang about the mundane lifestyle and the hope for a better life in a far-off place. Except for Nadia's character, it looked like reality, which brought depth to the surfaced tune. She was unwittingly predicting her own fate.

Nicholas followed Nadia's every move and was enamoured of her. He could not believe her talent and felt like a star-struck fan. He was amazed by how it all had worked out for her, including those evenings

and days of training. Voice and dancing were key, and she easily sur-
passed those skills. He enjoyed the entire play, including her cosying
up to her companion when being convinced to leave. He could see that
it was staged and understood the imagery of theatre.

He looked at Amelie, who nodded in agreement. They were so
impressed by her skills and were proud that she was back in her field.
Nadia was comfortable in the theatre and confident in herself.

Nicholas had to go backstage at the intermission.

"Brava, brava," he said as he entered Nadia's dressing room.

"Thank you, darling. And the flowers are lovely."

"Glad that you like them. You are truly amazing out there. And so
talented. I had no idea that you were that great."

"Thank you. That is why you are here, dear, to see me at work," she
replied charmingly.

"Well, I am sure glad I came. And the children love it. They can't
wait to see you later at dinner."

"Of course, I may be a few minutes late. A little bit of press, and
then I will be right over after the show."

"Right, dear. Please sign these for them. We will see you later."

"Perfect. See you later."

She got back into character and finished Act III onstage. It was
the penultimate act, and she had to be energetic for the denouement,
the final scene when her character says goodbye and heads to a city
of bright lights and the final chorus. It was a crowd-pleaser as they
tapped around to what was reminiscent of an actual Broadway scene
and with the stage transformed to a New York City side street with
bright marquees. The crowds gave a standing ovation as the curtain
fell for the final time.

"Right, folks. Let's get across the street for dinner. Nadia says
that she will be a few minutes late. We can have some champagne to
celebrate."

"Sounds great. It was a lovely show. I cannot believe that she has the starring role."

"I know, and she has worked very hard for it," responded Nicholas.

"I thought that she was amazing. I can't wait to tell her," added Jenny as they collected their belongings and left the theatre.

"Right. It is just across the street. Sammy's. There it is."

"Perfect. I am famished," added Amelie.

"Let's have something to celebrate then," added Hank.

The group wandered across the street in the crisp evening air. With scarves and trench coats for the brisk summer air, they wafted into the West End restaurant, where they had a reservation for a cosy table by the window for six. Nicholas ordered the bottle on ice, which the waiter would pour when he got a chance, and ordered some caviar for the table.

Nadia waltzed in very noticeably and found them all seated.

"Congratulations, darling. You did it!" Nicholas exclaimed as she approached and kissed him on the cheek.

"Thank you, dear," she replied proudly.

"It was amazing. Congratulations," added Jenny.

"Hear! Hear! Brava. It was fantastic," chimed in Hank.

"I loved it, and you were perfect. It must have taken ages to learn your lines," added Amelie.

"It was so much hard work, and we were all very nervous tonight," Nadia admitted.

"You were perfect. It's a great show. I hope that it does very well," added Lars.

"Thank you, and so do we," she replied.

"Champagne, dear?" Nicholas asked as he reached to top up her flute.

"Lovely, darling," she responded.

"A toast, to Nadia. May you have a successful show," said Nicholas.

"Thank you, dear."

"To Nadia," they all said in unison.

"To Nadia, and may she have a long run of the show," added Hank.

They celebrated happier times and were all elated. It was the perfect summer evening, and the case was behind them. They could live life in the open without any fear of being followed. The champagne flowed, and they ordered their mains and desserts. Before they knew it, it was after midnight and they were on coffee and a cheese platter. They were celebrating the evening. Nadia kept her scarf on to protect her throat from the draft. She looked the part of the star and felt as if she were beginning again.

Nicholas would be off to the island the following week while Nadia stayed and performed, and then she would have a week with him at the end of the summer before heading back to finish the show before the fall. They hoped to wrap up in October and perhaps do a stint on Broadway by the following spring. It was all up in the air. The couple rested after a long evening on the settee in the living room in Mayfair. She had a busy summer ahead of her with rehearsals and late nights at the theatre. He did not seem to mind and was worried about her being alone with only Mildred to help when he was gone.

"Are you sceptical about my career move?" she asked.

"Not really. It was something that you have done before, and you are very talented," he answered reassuringly.

"Thank you, darling. That means the world to me. I need your full support."

"You have it every step of the way."

"It will be hard next week without you, coming home to an empty house in the evenings."

"Try to keep some company. It won't be too long before I am back. My parents are getting fragile."

"I will try," she promised despondently, knowing what it was like to return to an empty house late at night during their early days. Having him at home kept her grounded. Or else she would be with her castmates on their evening excursions after the play.

"If you need a break, come, but it won't be too long before you see my parents again."

"No, not too long. It is just that I feel so restricted with my heavy schedule. I have commitments now until next spring. How will we manage when I am in New York?"

"We will manage as we always do. It is only for a short while, and I will travel in. We will find you a lovely apartment overlooking the Hudson right near the theatre. Now why don't we go this Thanksgiving when the play wraps and look at places?"

"You always know just how to say the right things."

"Yes, dear." He was exhausted and drew her closer.

It was a beautiful summer's evening. The open windows drew in fresh night air and they gazed upon the quaint side street where activity could be heard as revelers of the evening walked home.

Amelie awoke to a Sunday in Knightsbridge. There was a calm before the week began. She read the morning papers and glanced at her rock of Gibraltar as his ash brown hair sprawled the pillow. She let him slumber as she searched for more activities for their trip. It will be a trip to remember. Their lives were going at such a fast pace and they would not have the chance to have another trip. The summer was waning and before they knew it would be over. The neighbourhood was shedding its regulars for the summer residents and changing the feel of the summer to more of a shopping vibe. She thought about their last week at the country house and then brisk October and that familiar feeling of a new term for many and its optimism.

"Morning, dear," he said as he awoke.

"Morning. Would you like anything? I can make us some lovely strawberry and banana smoothies."

"Sounds lovely," he said as he turned, barely awake.

"Are you going in today?"

"A bit later, I suppose."

"Right then. Coffee?"

"Sure."

Amelie thought he needed a good espresso and a protein shake to get him moving. Marietta was on holiday that week. It would be like the old days, just the two of them. She enjoyed the private moments. She left and walked to the kitchen, where she found everything properly placed to use.

"Fabulous," she murmured as she sliced and diced, scooped and blended. She hoped that a cosy morning in would relieve any tension between them from that old case that had caused so much tension. She recalled the stress on her end and his soothing advice, and her father and brother's constant updates and time away from Lars's workload. This should really be their time. She had so much to make up to him, especially after the situation with Jude, who was an absolute newcomer from Lars's point of view and was competing for the "knight in shining armour" title.

Lars accepted the olive branch as he cautiously sipped his coffee and then gulped down his smoothie. There were years of experience between them, and there were many Sunday morning reconciliations just like this one. He knew the routine and would play his role most dedicatedly.

"Right then. I have to get ready for the office. I have to plan for the trip, and then we can have that vacation you want."

"Oh no. Do not go yet. I was just getting used to having you here," she pleaded.

"I am sorry, but I have to. I have an early morning meeting and then the flight. Will call you from work later."

"OK," she said reasonably.

He dragged himself out of bed and picked out his clothes from the closet

"I am sure that you have loads to do with Mrs Somerville and then Mr Mitchvale. Planning a trip to New York must be thrilling for you."

"It is. I am making new contacts at the same time."

"Right you are." He appeared and leant over to kiss her on the forehead. "Bye, darling."

"Bye. Talk to you later."

"Cheerio."

She heard him clamber down the stairs. She was not sure that her strategy had worked. She had more planning of her own to do.

"I see, Dad. The case has finally ended, and we are now free to live our lives completely."

"That is right, dear. All over and done. I have heard from Jude, and he has now settled in to his regular routine and has put this behind him and the business," he consoled her.

"Perfect. How has he been?"

"Just fine. He sends his best to you and Lars and hopes that you will have a trip over sooner rather than later."

"Yes. Thanks. We will have to see. We are off to Bordeaux when Lars returns from Malta."

"Great news. I am off to see my parents, and then Nadia will follow."

"Will she?"

"Yes. A short break before the fall season starts, and then off to

New York next spring. I suppose that you can help her to manage that. I shall be travelling in to see her."

"I would be delighted. I have just the place for her in the Theater District. It should be an amazing experience for her."

"Right you are, dear. Right you are."

"Well, have a glorious trip to Nan's. Send them my love, and tell them that I will see them soon."

"I will, dear. Take care of yourself until Lars comes back, and enjoy the French countryside."

"It should be marvellous this time of the year."

"It will be so beautiful. I can imagine it."

Chapter 11

Summer Sun

Amelie and Lars arrived by train to the quaint town. There were cobbled streets and ancient brick structures with winding streets encircling the little village and leading to the chateau. Aunt Marguerite's chateau was in the vicinity; however, Amelie chose to stay at a quaint apartment in the village which was catered by the management. She relished the option to cycle to the *boulangerie* and buy her goodies to take back the apartment as they whiled the days away in the ambience and amid the summer sunset, sipping wine in the evenings until the sun dipped below the horizon at 9 p.m.

The next day she had planned a cycle through the neighbouring champagne vineyard. She and Lars had once ridden through the manicured lanes until they reached the quaint chalet where the operations were managed.

"Do you remember any of this from the last time?"

"Yes." He nodded as he followed her through the vines and down the dusty track to the chalet.

"Who owns it?"

"I have no idea who manages it all now. Let's have lunch a bit farther down underneath that tree."

"Perfect." He felt as if all his stress had been lifted and he was in another hemisphere without technology and the stress from the office.

"Right here looks good," she assessed as they rode closer to the area.

"It's fine."

They stopped and dismounted their bikes, which they leant against a mahogany tree. Amelie used the branches as shade from the searing sun and laid out a chequered tablecloth with baguettes, cheese, and more wine. A fabulous tarte Tatin was also laid out for dessert. Lars laid his head on the soft grass in the shade and stared at the sky while he bit into the hard crust.

"It is much cooler here," she commented. "I had no idea that it would still be so warm in the middle of September."

"It usually is on the Continent. Luckily we have some canned air at the flat."

"Luckily. I searched high and low to make sure, just in case."

"Brava to you, dear."

"Thanks."

"Are you enjoying it all?"

"Wonderful. It feels like old times, when we were at uni and would come to visit your family and stay in the town so that we could have time to ourselves in the evenings."

"I know. It is so special. I knew that you would like it here."

"I do. Very much. I also needed it. I started to feel the work and the stress. The case in Malta seems to be going on for ages."

"I know. At least the other case is over."

"At least. But we do not need to talk about that now."

"No," she agreed as she nestled closer to him in the shade.

They wiled away the rest of afternoon, tucked beneath the oak tree and reminiscing of times that were memorable to them. The rest of the day they walked the bikes along dusty winding paths through the vineyards to the stately chateau and stopped to have another view of a landmark they had seen before.

They toured the historical site, walking through creaky corridors to ornate rooms which seemed eclipsed by time. Ornaments and pottery of gold and china were on display, once belonging to the previous occupants and now preserved for history. Four-poster beds with antique quilts and cushions in regal colours set the character of the room beneath crystal chandeliers and antique oil paintings of the Renaissance and other periods. Special characteristics of the room depicted the personality of the occupants of a bygone era. Gone were the days of state visits and luxurious parties, of riding in the hills on horses and hunting in the nearby forest. What remained was the riding gear and carriage particles used on long journeys. Tapestried murals of historical life lined the walls, where cherubs and other fairies were in permanent view of the elaborate tales of yesteryear.

Amelie had a sense of purpose as she viewed the delicate, orderly interior. She had centred herself after an arduous summer.

"It is all so very well preserved, almost like how they left it. Do you get that feeling?"

"Most certainly. Look, there is even the brush that they once used. And the gold comb and dishes for washing on the vanity."

"I know. I can almost sense them and get the feeling that they are watching."

"I doubt it, dear. They have been gone at least a century now—and even longer for the first inhabitants. This chateau was built in the fifteenth century."

"I know. Look at the wonderful artwork on display."

"I suppose that they would have known the artists. Look, some of these are portraits."

The painting he pointed to was of the lady of the house. It must have been done in the 1800s. She was dressed in a delicate blue silk gown with a draped collar and had small dandelions over her ear. A large pendant was centred in the middle of her collar with her dusky brown hair tied back. She had enthralling doe-like blue eyes, the epitome of innocence and of a noblewoman.

"I suppose that she had a major ball to attend that evening or had been dragged from her morning ride to sit in attendance and have the painting finished," Amelie noted jovially.

"I suppose. And look at him." Lars pointed to the painting of a nobleman obviously done at the same time. He was dressed in a red waistcoat and white breeches. "He looks like he was made for outdoor country life."

"Yes. There is something very courageous about him. I think we may have just seen his room. I wonder what it must have been like not knowing that your possessions would be on view one day?"

"I know. It is a bit intrusive."

"I think so. To have strangers come in day after day to analyse your life."

"That is right. I suppose they may have expected it, being aristocrats and public people."

"I suppose. If it will make you feel better, I want to see our art on display at the museum. We have certainly been through too much to keep it all."

"I think so. I did not know that you were such an aficionado."

"Of course. I have been for a long time. Growing up around it all, I feel like a natural. And then I studied a bit."

"I see. Do you feel inspired by it?"

"Yes. I certainly do. Even now I feel very enthused just by being here."

"I guess there is a saying: 'to the manor born'."

"I guess." She played it off. However, she felt in her element, and it reminded her of her grandfather Louis Eric and how they spent afternoons looking at paintings and his historical accounts behind them. It took her back to summers with her mother at their own chateau and the familiarity and security that Amelie had felt. "I think that I needed this, to come close to our home and to soak it all in before getting back to that hectic schedule."

"Take all the time that you need, dear."

"I do wonder how Dad is getting along with Nan and Granddad?"

"I suppose very well as usual. There is nothing to worry about. He should be back for more nights at the theatre, I suppose," Lars stated candidly.

Amelie blushed. "I suppose. That is his life now. Who would have thought?"

"Things do change. I remember those lovely picnics on the grounds here in France with your parents."

"So do I, dear. So do I."

She did not want to reflect on how their lives had changed. Her father was out of his comfort zone, as was she. She was trying to hold onto whatever remnants there were.

"It is getting late. The sun is beginning to dim. We should head back to the hotel," Lars said.

"Let's. It has been wonderful," she agreed.

It had been a day well spent and a day of closeness between them. The evening proved to be even better as they sat at a cosy table at the bistro and ordered their favourite meals. Amelie started with the *soupe à l'oignon*, and Lars had the prosciutto wraps with a vintage Chardonnay for the table. The sun had almost set, and the candles provided the perfect ambiance.

"There is just something about being here that I cannot get anywhere else," she noted.

"I know. It is unique, and it brings back so many memories."

"Do tell. Like what?"

"All the times that we spent here and made wonderful memories. This is all a part of you and me," he admitted, hoping that he had gotten it right.

"Really. That is fabulous. Thank you. We need to come more often." She was pleased that her plan had worked and that she had rekindled the spark in her marriage that was dampening. It took work. She had to admit it: there was no one else she would rather be with. They indulged in the decadent mille feuille as Amelie sipped the last of the wine in her glass.

"Shall we retire?" Lars offered.

"I think we shall," she concurred.

Nicholas arrived on the island close to teatime. The car drove him to the house on the hill. His parents were seated on the settee on the veranda, eagerly awaiting his arrival. The car stopped on the curved driveway, and he disembarked with his hand case. The driver collected his suitcase and placed it on the veranda.

"Good afternoon, Mum, Dad," Nicholas greeted them.

"Hello, dear. How was your flight?"

"Great. I thought that I would come straight here and see you before stopping off at the villa."

"That is not a problem," replied Lionel.

"Dad, you are looking great. And, Mum, you look lovely."

"Thank you. Come and have a drink with us."

"Sure. The flights are not like they used to be. I could use some tea and some wonderful cakes and cream," he admitted.

"Verena will be out with that shortly. Come and sit here."

"The driver should be back in a few hours. I am sure that they have filled the fridge at the house."

"I am sure. But there is nothing like a home-cooked meal. Now come and tell us, how are the children?"

"They are fine. Amy has finally gotten over that ordeal, and the case is now closed. Hank is looking after his family wonderfully, and Lance has been given the all-clear. The summer is wrapping up on a good note. Also, Nadia has done brilliantly in the show and will be heading to Broadway in the spring. So I will be able to visit more as we will be closer."

"Sounds terrific." Winnie remained hopeful.

"I do hope that it will all work out for her."

"So do we. Will she be coming soon?" asked Lionel.

"No, not until the holidays. And then we will head to the Big Apple so she can rehearse."

"Perfect. It all is lovely. I am so happy that Amy is now settling into her old routine. It took us awhile to get her uplifted."

"Yes. We thought that she would not cope. Then something twisted, and it worked out fine. It always does with her."

"I know. There is strength somewhere. I hope that her life will be normal. It has been very difficult for her. Jude Deneuve, son of Clyde, was actually the missing link in the whole ordeal. He was able to offer the information to finally solve the case."

"That is interesting. I have not heard that name in a long time."

"I know. It was a blast from the past. Apparently Lou had an agreement which fell through, and Margaux decided not to go through with it. It was the bank that had relied on the third-party sale who were the culprits, committing fraud on the client portfolio for years and trying to reclaim the assets. Such an ordeal with it all coming from high up. I can safely say that it is the end of the summer and there is no more need to worry. Obviously Amy was targeted because she was a beneficiary, and they assumed she would have the documents."

"It is amazing that for decades someone could claim ownership," commented Lionel.

"I know. For years unbeknown to us. At least Marguerite and me. Who knows if Margaux ever suspected anything."

"Absolutely. I suppose with her aptitude she might have," noted Winifred.

"I think she may have and considered it all water under the bridge."

"So how did Amy take to having this stranger appear?" asked Winifred.

"At first she was reticent and did not want anything to do with it, and then she took to it very well. They actually get along well, which her aunt did not find amazing."

"I think that Lars was a bit perplexed over it."

"Oh no," she added.

"Yes, It was very unusual. You see, he was not there when our lives were different and there were so many people in our lives, including Clyde and Lou, and holidays and parties."

"It may have been a bit too close for comfort," she added while Lionel nodded.

"I know, Mummy. I know." Nicholas's voice cracked at the thought that Amelie had suffered from their closeness, that she bore the brunt of the relationship in a negative way and it had changed her. "I think that she is a bit jaded from it all. I don't know if she will be the same with the naiveté and values that she once had. She may have the notion that there will always be something underlying beneath the facade."

"Not to worry. That is life. You have to know how to protect yourself when it happens again. And experience is the best teacher," Winifred reasoned.

"I do suppose. But not having Margaux to answer ..." His voice almost cracked.

"I know. Luckily you had Jude to testify. But what do you think she could have answered?"

"I have no idea. Perhaps it is my insecurity. I may be no better off than Lars—an outsider to that way of life and all that history."

"No. No. She loved you. The years that she had spent visiting here. You knocked her off her feet, and she fell in love with you and never looked back. No other person or past could take your place. I knew her. She would never let anything get in between you and her. She made her choice, and her choice was you and with us and her children."

"Don't think like that. It is over. All over. She has left you the best that anyone can, and we have so much to thank her for, including her having touched our lives the way that she did," added Lionel.

"The wonderful parties, birthdays, christenings, weddings, and style. The glamourous style that she had. It still lingers in her interior decoration of her homes, and her traditions, and her sister who is such an integral part of this family. She was so candid and experienced. You can never lose that."

"I know, Mother. I guess that I am being foolish."

"Don't worry, dear. It happens to us all."

"Let me get Verena to bring the tea. It will be great to see her. She has been like a second mum," he joked.

Winifred laughed. She knew that she was no whizz in the kitchen and was grateful to have had such a talented chef for decades.

Verena brought out a tray of tea and delicate cakes, along with pastries and sandwiches, and placed it in front of them.

"It looks delicious. Thank you. All this for me?" Nicholas asked.

"Yes. We think that you are special," she answered.

"Why, thank you. It is always lovely to be back."

They served it up and tucked into the items from the tray. Nicholas passed the afternoon with his two-favourite people. He also got the woe off his chest and felt relieved. It was just what he needed. Even If Marguerite had more answers, they were not necessary for him to have. The summer sun was still at a high point, and the jet lag was setting in. Nicholas knew that it was time to get to the villa and settle in for the evening. He no longer had the vigour that he'd had as a younger man. When travelling with children, he and Margaux would go to the beach after the plane landed. He was surrounded by memories and a new stint in New York would be best for him. The week was filled with activities with Lionel and Winifred. There were a few soirées with friends who had travelled in after having been gone for ages as well, former locals whom he had not seen all year but who travelled in at the end of summer just to fly out as was customary when they were off to study in the autumn.

There was the autumn and the freshness that it brought, the changing of the colours of the leaves, and the cool and crisp mornings. He yearned for London and those autumns of getting the children back to school and having new meetings and clients in the city. He would acquiesce into it all. Now he had a new life of theatre and West End evenings to look forward to. Life was changing. Perhaps leaving it all behind was best. It was the gift that he'd been given, and he had to make the most of it. He called Nadia as she would be just ending the show.

"Hello, darling. I am just checking in."

"Hello. We are just wrapping up for the evening. I thought that I would go with a few of the cast to the pub across the street rather than be lonely tonight," she commented.

"Yes, splendid idea. Make sure to get home safely. I miss you already. Wish that you could have made that weekend here."

"I know. But we have more to do with the production to make it marketable for the Big Apple. It was a last-minute change. But you shall be back soon enough, and then we have New York."

"That's right. Lovely. Speak to you soon. Bye."

"Bye, darling. Miss you."

He was stranded on the island for a week without her. The time usually flew by. Once he discovered how to keep busy, it should go well. It was important to see his family as they were getting older and time with them was valuable.

The villa was set in a very exclusive area near the water. It had a whitewashed tropical decor. He and Nadia had loads of souvenirs and memorabilia from when they had just started out. Her special characteristics were everywhere, and there were no memories of Margaux. They'd spent more time at the house with the children, where they could entertain on the patios and take the children for walks along the shoreline. He would spend the next few days boating with friends and visiting the house. He felt revived after the conversation with his parents. He tried to keep his mind off it and thought about the week ahead and pure relaxation.

"Shall I take these downstairs?" asked Lars as he collected the last of the bags.

"Yes, I am ready now. We should try to avoid the Sunday afternoon rush back to London."

"Sure thing. I will see you downstairs. I will just pack these in the car."

"Thanks, dear. See you out front."

Lars found the tiny lift at the end of the corridor and descended to the lobby, where he stopped to finalise the bill. Amelie followed a few minutes later. She waved to the staff and entered the car, which was waiting in front.

"I am so sad that it is all over."

"I know. We still have a lovely drive back. We can perhaps have lunch near Dover as a final weekend break."

"That would be lovely. It will be chillier there, as you know, it is near the end of September."

"Yes. Have you your sweater, or is it out back?"

"It is out back, I think."

"Don't worry. I will get it later," she responded. "It is still bright and sunny here."

"Right then. Let's go."

Amelie felt the closeness that she always felt. She managed to rekindle the flame that had dimmed. She knew that the trip would work. She faced an optimistic autumn and was eager to get back to her usual routine. The drive was long as they wound through the tiny roads in the countryside. Closer to the afternoon, they could see the tunnel and the prospect that home was close. She relished the moment with the two of them. She basked in Lars's undivided attention. It was definitely the end of the season, which meant the turning over of a new leaf and the start of a new season.

Nadia had a new sensation as she left the theatre. She felt invigorated after the final curtain and hearing the applause. Their efforts had not been fruitless, and the long nights were not in vain. Her home was still empty as Nicholas was not due back until the weekend. It was a Sunday night.

"Coming along for drinks?" asked Chrissy, her colleague.

"Sure, why not?"

"It will be fab," responded Augusto, her theatre husband.

"Are you coming, Anabelle?"

"Sure. Let's go, shall we?" Annabelle replied.

"Is Nick still away?"

"Yes, until next week."

"Not to worry. You can hang out with us. No use going home to an empty flat," responded Chrissy.

"I know. He is so understanding."

"Sounds like you have hit jackpot," commented Annabelle.

"I surely have," Nadia responded proudly.

"I can have you to myself this week," joked Augusto.

"Not a problem," she joked back.

"Now what are you all having? The first round is on me," Augusto asked as he turned to the counter while they each took a seat.

They placed their orders and sat in the corner seat, placing their bags near their feet. The world around them had wound down, and their evening was just beginning. They would soon need to move on to another, more convenient place once the pub had closed.

"I wonder how Nick is getting on?"

"Don't worry. He can take care of himself," consoled Chrissy.

"I am sure that he is fine. You never stop worrying. Now just think how different life will be when we tour New York."

"I am sure. Nick is so excited."

"I am too. I have already warned all my friends," expressed Annabelle.

"Life will be fabulous," Chrissy added.

"I can't wait to get a bite of the Big Apple," replied Nadia.

"Here we are, five pints," offered Augusto as he grasped the four glasses and placed them on the table.

"Thank you, darling," responded Annabelle.

"Thank you," added Nadia and Chrissy.

"Now what have I missed?"

"We were talking about the Big Apple."

"Oh, I am so up for it. I cannot wait," he responded as he sang in tune.

"Yes, we can't wait," joined Chrissy.

"But we still have to get through the season here. The holidays will be packed," said Annabelle.

"Packed. I am so excited because I will travel, and then we'll get to New York for rehearsals."

"Sure. It will be cold in February," added Chrissy.

"Freezing in February. We had better prepare for those nor'easters," responded Augusto.

"Gosh, we will have to walk around in those massive arctic coats," added Chrissy.

"I am sure that we will be fine," commented Annabelle.

"Mm, yes," agreed Augusto.

"So where are you going first? Are you going to see Nick's family?" asked Chrissy.

"Yes. We holiday on the island every year. His parents are there, and the other family will visit."

"Sounds lovely. Why don't you take us?" asked Chrissy.

"You are welcome to come along."

"Gee, thanks. We might just take you up on it." Chrissy was impressed.

"Yes. I could do with a nice break in warmer weather," added Annabelle.

"What a perfect idea," noted Augusto.

"Actually it would be."

"There. All done," confirmed Augusto.

They sipped their drinks until the last call and then wandered up the street to the wine bar.

It was a warm Sunday afternoon. Nick was docking the boat with a few friends from childhood.

"Wonderful day out," he commented.

"Thanks, old chap. Mel and I had a great time. She is gathering the things below deck."

"How long have I known you now, Bruce?"

"I cannot remember that long ago. It was that summer that you came down. We might have been about twelve."

"Gosh. Time sure does fly. We spent that summer fishing and on the shores."

"Nick, we were so young and had the whole world ahead of us. If we knew then what we know now, how would you have done it differently?"

"I do not know. It is hard to say. I would have loved Margaux more. I think that is the only thing I would have changed. How about you?"

"More times like these with good friends. And you are right. Mel and I have been together a long time. At the end of the day, it all boils down to one thing, and that is to love the ones you are with."

"Life has taught me a great lesson, and now I have a second chance. I never would have seen this happening. I expected it to be forever. I have left it now as water under the bridge and take all the moments I can whenever I can."

"No regrets, my friend. No regrets."

They tied the boat to the dock and carried the bags from the deck to the cars.

"What do you say? How about coming to our club for dinner?"

"Sure. I could use some company." Nick followed them back to the club and continued catching up with his lifelong friends.

There was a strong sense of nostalgia as the wind blew from the ocean towards the outdoor patio, where tables were set in lace and fine crystal. Without Nadia, it took him back to the previous days of outdoor parties and old friends celebrating with him and Margaux. It was amazing how often those times seemed to be encapsulated in moments which surfaced after much exhilaration. Margaux still had a strong hold on him, even from the grave. He drove back to the villa and noticed that Nadia had not checked her WhatsApp with it being almost 2.30 a.m. in the UK, but he was exhausted and went to sleep.

Nadia had a late night and took a taxi from the West End to Mayfair where she safely entered and took the lift to the flat. She checked her phone again. There were no messages from Nick. She nestled on the sofa under the blankets and fell asleep.

Chapter 12

Back to Routine

A melie and Lars awoke that Monday in their own room. It was a fresher morning and the end of September. It was cool and cosy with the blue interior and closed drapes. The aroma of cinnamon and bread for breakfast being baked by Marietta downstairs emanated throughout the room.

"Smells delicious," Amelie said as turned towards Lars.

"Yes. I must get up. We have meetings all morning," he answered.

"Sure, darling. I have to get in early myself."

"We have to eat something, though," he admitted.

"Yes. We had better."

He crawled out of bed and went to the bathroom.

"We need another summer," she stated.

"Afraid it is over now, my sweet."

"At last. And I survived it."

"You sure did."

"I need to see if Dad got back safely," she said.

"Yes. Tell him I said hello."

"I will. I will call him later. I have so many people to check on today."

"So do I," he said, bemused, as he closed the door.

She checked her emails and photos on Instagram. Nicholas had a few up from the trip on the boat and some with friends. She was impressed by how his life had improved and was worried that she would miss them next winter.

"Do you think that we should go to New York to visit them?"

"Yes. But we have so much to consider before then. The holidays will be right bang in the middle of it all."

"You are right. We will have to think of it later," she answered, a bit disappointed by his answer.

"Right then," he said as he exited the washroom. "Shall we go downstairs and get some breakfast? I am starving."

"Sure, dear. I will be right down."

She turned and flipped through the photos. It felt like the end of summer and the beginning of the work year.

Amelie rolled up to the office and entered the building. Her staff had been in early, getting their reports together for the updates on her clients. Mr Mitchvale had started his trip to New York, and Mrs Somerville had just left Kenya, while the others were interested in more local trips and events. Bernita wanted to visit the Highlands, and Quincy wanted an eco-tourism Finnish trip. The staff were thrilled to assist people with their dreams.

Delianna was seated when Amelie entered her office. "Good morning. It is such lovely day. Wonderful to see you."

"Good morning, all. Wonderful to see you too. Yes, it is a lovely autumnal day, and I am sure that my desk is loaded," responded Amelie.

"Yes. However, I have sorted through the most pertinent so that you can find it easily."

"Thanks. I appreciate it. Now just one cup of coffee, please, to start the day."

"Sure. In a few minutes," Delianna responded as she left her desk to go the kitchen.

Amelie walked in and it was very orderly and clean. The room was at a perfect temperature and was cool with grey and beige tones from the decorating. Amelie opened the blinds to see the perfect picture of a morning in Knightsbridge. She turned on the PC and sorted through the bills on the table. She came across administrative envelopes which were necessary to run the business and to overcome the bureaucratic hurdles of doing business in London. She had gone through it all and had a timetable precisely set up to meet the due dates. Her emails included some from new clients looking for relocation assistance, one from Nadia about her move to New York, and some from clients who were thrilled with their trips. It gave Amelie such a sense of accomplishment to read through the feedback. She came across an email from Jude:

Dear Amelie,

I hope that you have had a wonderful summer eventually and are back to your routine. I am very sorry about what you have had to experience this summer and was happy to assist with the case. I do hope that there won't be any more problems. I hope to travel to London next month, and I look forward very much to calling on the family. I will keep you posted. I have someone whom I would love for you to meet.

Best,
Jude

Amelie was pleased to hear from him and was curious as to who the person might be. It was probably a friend or a romantic interest. She didn't think that he would bring anyone who was insignificant. She grew perturbed and cast the thought aside so that she could concentrate on her work.

She also got a message from Hank, who had been to the South of France:

> Hello, Amelie,
>
> I will have to pop in for lunch when I come to the city. We had a lovely time in France. Uncle Lance is coming along very well. You must try to see them once things calm down at work. Aunt Marguerite would be happy to see you. The investigation has closed and the injunctions ordered. You should not have any more to worry about.
>
> Your brother,
> Hank John

She smiled when she read his message. Finally it was all over. Perhaps that is why Jude had contacted her?

Amelie tried not to spend any more time as the ordeal had brought a great void into her life as it was. At least she could walk the streets and not worry about her account being hacked. She wondered if Nicholas knew. He was due back any day from the island.

She perused the site for New York properties and contacts from her real estate days. She wanted to set her family up in a very convenient location, where she could also visit if needed, perhaps a lovely two-bedroom loft overlooking the river near the Theater District. Nadia would be in Midtown every day.

Nicholas ordered a car from Heathrow and arrived in Mayfair early on Friday. Nadia was awake and waiting for him. She hugged him as soon as she saw him.

"Hello, dear. This time it has been difficult without you. I do not know how we will bear being apart this winter."

"Hello, darling. Lovely to see you. I will be visiting very often."

"How was your flight?"

"Had a great flight that could have been shorter as I needed to see you."

"Fantastic to hear. I have been waiting here for you."

"Perfect."

"Are you hungry? There is some food in the microwave."

"Lovely."

"We had a great week of the show. A standing ovation every night. Spent a few evenings with the cast and had some lonely nights."

"Not to worry; I am here now," he answered apologetically. Apologetic because he had not concentrated on his marriage, had been stuck in the past, and had felt as though he had not appreciated Nadia. He felt refreshed after confiding in his parents, and he'd made a pact with himself to be more attentive. "We shall make it all up over the next few months," he promised.

"Lovely, darling. Amelie has been busy with the preparations for New York. I cannot wait. Also, I hope that it would be all right if I asked some of the cast to the holidays with us. It won't put us out too much, will it?"

"No, not at all. We shall be lucky to have them. Now let me just take a quick look at my messages, and we can have a meal."

Nicholas took some time to settle into his den and to go over his correspondence. He noticed that Mr Hoover had sent his invoice for services rendered. It was a hefty cost, but it was worth it. Finally the investigation was concluded, and the culprits would be brought to justice with the family heirlooms intact.

Nicholas entered the kitchen to heat the pie. "Darling, are you having some?" he asked.

Nadia had vanished to the sitting room to go over her lines and voice. "Just a little salad, dear," she answered.

"All right." He prepared the small salad and carried the bowls to the table.

"Perfect, dear. Thank you." She felt pampered.

"Anything for you. Now I think that we should plan a weekend to New York to see the flats. I can ask Amy to get it all sorted."

"Perfect. I have missed you."

"I have missed you too."

Amelie found the perfect place and set up a viewing in two weeks' time. She knew that properties left the market as soon as they arrived in New York, so she'd had to negotiate a fee in advance. It was a penthouse suite overlooking the Hudson River. Her day had been long, and it was time to pack it in and head back to the flat. She almost wished that it was her going, but she and Lars would have ample time to visit Nicholas and Nadia in New York. *New York,* she thought. *How times have changed.* The horizons and network for the family was expanding even more, and business was back to normal after the tumultuous summer. Fond memories existed of country walks and matches, boat rides and travel, and the dirt path through the vineyard in France to supersede the bad. Out of the bad came the Good Samaritan and family friend Jude and the reinstatement of Amelie's feelings for Lars. Fall had turned a new leaf of consistency and an even balance needed to coordinate the end of the year.

"Hello, dear. I am just on my way home. Are you working late?"

"No. I will be home in time for dinner. What is there?"

"I think that Marietta has some ratatouille. Is that all right?"

"Perfect. A perfect meal with you in about an hour."

"Lovely, see you at home."

She did not want to tell him about the email. She figured that Jude had found someone and there would be no more issues. Her life was full with Lars; however, Jude would always hold a place that was private. She walked and let the crisp autumnal air comb her fair hair. It was now past her shoulders and gently whisked her face.

Nicholas and Nadia entered the club-class cabin for the excursion to New York. They sat facing each other and settled into their chairs. Nadia was excited. She had not visited New York many times before, and Nicholas had last visited a few years ago. They were offered champagne, which they accepted, sipping it before take-off.

"Lovely, isn't it?" she said as she crossed her long legs in cream leggings and comfortable Uggs.

"Yes. I love these transatlantic flights. Are you comfortable?"

"Yes. Very." She placed her glass on the side tray and gathered her long blonde locks together to tie in a ponytail. "Look at the menu. What do you fancy eating?"

"I think that the Welsh lamb looks good. Also the chocolate mousse cake."

"Yes. I am watching my figure. I think that I will have the fish and lentils. Look, there is Eton mess."

"Sounds divine. I think that I will have the Eton mess as well. Anyway, we had better secure our trays for take-off."

The stewardess collected the glasses and checked the tray tables and seat belts. Nadia was careful to do everything properly. She looked opposite her at Nicholas and smiled.

He smiled back. "We should be getting in at about 8 p.m. local time. It is a rather quick flight of seven hours."

"Wonderful. Just in time to settle in. What time will we reach the hotel?"

"I think that we will be there at about 9.30 if we are on schedule. There may be traffic getting into New York."

"I see. I guess we can go shopping tomorrow?"

"I suppose. But we have appointments with the estate agency. We can do whatever you want after that. We can take a tour of the park, or you can go to the spa. Whatever you wish."

"Sounds delightful. There are so many movies. What do you think that you will watch?"

"I do not know, dear. I think that I will just tune into the proms or something and relax until they serve dinner. Do you want something to read?"

"No thanks. I think that I will just wait for the entertainment to start."

"Lovely, dear."

She put her head on the pillow and waited for take-off. The taxi was rather long. Finally the plane lifted off and they were airborne. She looked across and smiled at her husband. The meals were brought rather quickly so that they could get some rest. The passengers were served with an appetiser and then the main meal with rolls and some wine.

"I won't drink any more," Nadia admitted. "I hear that alcohol and jet lag do not mix."

"No, they do not. We will have something at the Ritz. There is a lovely suite waiting."

"Amy has done such a good job getting this planned for us. We must get her a special gift from here. I saw a lovely pair of earrings from Saks online."

"That would be lovely. She will really like that."

"I know," she replied, pleased. Her and Nicholas's relationship was very good as they were less than a decade in age apart. In relation to Amelie, she felt more like an older cousin or young aunt than a stepmother.

They sat back and enjoyed the flight while the dessert and cheese were served. Then the cabin lights dimmed, and it was very restful for the remainder of the flight.

Nadia looked over at her husband, who was sleeping. He looked so relaxed and peaceful that she decided to occupy herself with her own entertainment. She was bursting with excitement and could not wait to land. It would soon be over, in an hour, and then the whole city awaited then.

Nicholas eventually turned over and she peered across the screen to smile at him. He smiled back.

"I had a good nap," he commented.

"I know. I have been up for most of it."

"Oh dear," he answered.

"I know. I will rest tonight though."

He looked a bit despondent. He had hoped for a sky-view meal on their first night. He supposed that they would just settle in and wait for a romantic breakfast in the morning in the suite. Nadia peered out her window as the plane was nearing the city. She could see the fabulous lights which were all lined up symmetrically. They looked like a show town at first.

"It looks wonderful. Look." She pointed.

"I see. And soon we will be in the heart of it." He enjoyed how candid and excited she was.

They disembarked and passed the security and customs to the baggage carousel. Luckily theirs were some of the first bags to come off as they were tagged priority. They exited the airport and jumped into a car that had been ordered to take them to Manhattan. They drove through the Queens Midtown Tunnel and then to the Upper East Side, where they crossed over to the park and drove in front of the hotel. The doormen, who were waiting because it was a late check-in, smoothly escorted them into the lobby and to the front desk. The suite had been prepared and was waiting for them.

Nadia walked in and saw a corridor with a large sitting room and a view of the city. The bathroom was a large walk-in with a shower and bathtub. She could not contain her excitement.

"I can't believe it. It is fabulous," she squealed as Nicholas tipped the baggage carrier, who then showed him a few of the appliances before leaving.

"I know. We can stay up all night if you want now." He laughed.

"I know. I am a bit tired, and we have a long day. I think that I will unpack a few things."

"Do you want anything?" he said as he opened the minibar.

"I am not that hungry. It is almost 3 a.m. our time. Sorry."

"That is fine. I think that I will have something and enjoy this wonderful view."

He felt as if he had come full circle. His marriage was in a good place, and he had gotten over the insecurities and unanswered issues regarding his previous marriage, as well as the case that had been hovering for three years. He felt as though he was finally starting anew and perhaps a new city was the place to be. He retrieved a small bottle of whisky and sat on the settee and marvelled at the view. Was it too late for him to start over? Somehow he felt as though he was the luckiest man in the world.

A few hours later they awoke completely famished. Nadia removed the mask from her face and sat up while he got up and opened the curtains.

"Looks like a bright and crisp fall day," he stammered.

"Yes. Gosh, I am hungry. I think I just crashed out here."

"I think you did. We had a long day. Shall we order something?"

"Perfect. What do you want?"

"Coffee and toast. Eggs, I suppose."

"OK. I'll have a protein smoothie with some toast. I still have to watch my figure."

"Wonderful. You look fine, darling. I will ring down."

He enjoyed their time together. It was just what they needed to bond after all those theatre nights.

The waiter rolled the tray into the suite and left it in the room near the bed. Nadia moved to the edge of the bed and sat up at the table while Nicholas moved a chair over. He poured the coffee and distributed the toast.

"Jam, dear?" he asked.

"Yes, please. Thanks."

"Eggs?" he offered.

"No thanks. I will just sip this. It has cereal powder."

"They smell good," he taunted.

"I am fine, dear," she reminded him.

"OK. We will go to the agent's first thing and then get some shopping done. Luckily we are close to everything at this hotel."

"I know. I cannot wait. I want to get something for Mum and Amy. She has been so helpful."

"Sure." He turned on the television and got a bit of the morning news before getting dressed for the day. He felt relaxed in cashmere and khakis, complete with a navy trench coat.

Nadia appeared in a cream outfit with a rust-coloured suede jacket and matching boots. Her hair appeared frosted in the light, and her skin glowed with added highlighter. They took the car to the agency and went to visit a building in Midtown West. Nadia was ecstatic the moment she walked in. It was a vast apartment with large open windows overlooking the river and marble counters in the open-plan kitchen. It had two very large bedrooms with walk-in closets. It was for the professional, with the comfort of a view of the flowing river, to return to late at night after work.

"I just love it, dear," she expressed. "It has so much space, and family can visit. We can entertain. And just look at the kitchen and appliances! I love this suite."

"It is fantastic though, isn't it? And a concierge downstairs. But there is one more to see, and then you can choose."

"Perfect."

They were driven to the Upper East Side near the park and closer to the Theater District and Radio City Music Hall. It was a traditional building with all the amenities. The apartment had smaller corridors and hardwood floors and was prewar with that New York apartment aroma reminiscent of earlier years in Nicholas's life when the children were little. It had a low view of the park, a smaller blue and white tiled kitchen, and prewar bathrooms. It was very old-money style. When passing in taxis, Margaux had always wanted to know what these ones looked like inside as they were always so classy and quaint with the old-fashioned elevators and dressed doormen.

"I think it is so sweet. It is almost like our place in Mayfair I suppose. There is a beautiful dining room set. I love the view. I am not sure, though."

"It has potential. How much is this one?" Nicholas asked the agent.

"It is ninety-five hundred dollars a month short term. It is on special offer because there are others available in the building. There are two bedrooms, two baths, and a powder room for guests, and there are fabulous schools close by," he offered.

"Not bad for the price. If we wanted a year's lease?"

"We could negotiate something for you. We have a good relationship with the owners."

Nadia had to choose between the promising new property which exuded modernity and the traditional residence east of the park that could potentially move her to another aspect of her life. She was not thinking of children or walks along the park. She wanted the bright lights of the Theater District and late nights with the cast, and space to entertain Amy and Lars, and Hank and the children. It was a tough choice between the woman she had always known and the woman she had come to be. She opted for the one where her life was an open book and there were vast views and dreams as far as the eye could see.

"Honey, I think I prefer the one in Midtown West," she admitted.

"I understand. It is also closer to Times Square and offices there— in case I have business."

"That can be arranged," the agent said. "I will have my assistant pull up the paperwork, and we can get started for the six-month rental. The lease can be renewed if you change your mind. And it is an excellent management company. Although it is a new building, they have been in the business for generations."

He shook Nicholas's hand, "Thank you. It has been a pleasure. And, Nadia, thank you for your business and we look forward to welcoming you to New York."

"Thank you for your time. It has been delightful seeing the apartments," she responded.

"You are welcome. Can I take you anywhere?"

"No, that is not necessary. We will walk to Fifth Avenue from here. We are not that far, are we?" responded Nicholas.

"No. Not that far at all. I will show you the direction. It is such a beautiful day." He escorted them downstairs and pointed to the edge of the park's entrance and then the buildings.

"Thank you. We will be in touch," Nicholas said. Then he and Nadia began their stroll and enjoyed the ambience. The weather was crisp, and there were sales along Fifth Avenue for the stretch between Veterans Day and Thanksgiving.

"Any more thoughts on the place?" he asked.

"I think that the first one is superb. The second one is fit for a different lifestyle, the type that we already have at home."

"Home. Sounds good. So you think that you will come home after this?" he asked.

"Definitely I will be coming home," she reassured him.

He knew that it was a gamble relocating for these months and that the worst could happen.

"Good. I will be waiting. The apartment should be available from the first of January, so we can settle you in after the holiday trip. You should be able to ship most of your clothes in advance," he advised.

"Or I can get new ones," she remarked as she passed the department store. "Let's head in, darling. There is a sale."

He followed as she whisked herself in the autumn breeze into the store with others also in the race to start.

"Where shall we begin?" he asked as he looked at the rush despondently.

"Handbags and accessories."

"Oh, right here."

"Then we can move our way up. I cannot believe these bargains."

"Yes. Sixty per cent off sounds rather inviting."

"Fabulous."

They spent the afternoon scouring the floors, until they left with three large shopping bags.

"We might need to buy an extra suitcase to get this all home," he suggested.

"Or we can have the hotel ship it or store it. I shall be back in six weeks."

"Marvellous idea. Surely you want that evening gown for the New Year's bash at the club."

"Surely," she replied giddily. "I just love those earrings we bought for Amy with her favourite stones."

"Yes. She will like those." Nicholas was miles away from the settled street in London he called home. He was in a fast-paced environment. He thought that perhaps his second wind was approaching.

"Shall we tell her?"

"No. Let's keep it as a surprise. We will give them to her when we get back. She must want to know how it all went. Let's take a photo." They huddled together, took a selfie in the bustle of Fifth Avenue, and sent it to Amelie via instant message. She replied with a few emoji. "There, you see. Brilliant. Now shall we have dinner on top of the rock. It has been a dream of mine to go back there."

"Certainly, Mr Mullbury. I thought that you would never ask."

They walked back to the hotel to drop off the things they'd bought and rest until dinner. Nicholas sipped an afternoon aperitif and ordered room service for lunch. "I think that we will have an early dinner. I am feeling the jet lag," he noted.

"Yes. We had better call the concierge."

"Right you are. Mind you, in my younger years I would have had to wait with my colleagues. Things are different now that I have reached a certain stage. I can nap when I want and work on my own schedule. I hope that you adjust quickly, as the first few weeks might be trying."

"I know. I think that I will have a small nap myself." They nestled in the warm room, closed the blinds to the light and the view, and rested.

"I heard from Dad and Nadia. Looks like things are going well for them," Amelie said as she showed Lars the photo of them huddled together on Fifth Avenue.

"They look happy. It was just what they needed. Did they get the flat?"

"Yes. The one on the west side. I thought that it would be just perfect for her. I figured that she would not want anything too traditional."

"Which would you have chosen?"

"I can't say. I liked them both. Probably the safer choice in case there was family. Why?

"I am just asking."

"You are not planning on relocating, are you?"

"No. At least not right now. It would be nice to visit them over there, though."

"Definitely. They leave after New Year's. I cannot believe how fast the year is going. The holiday decorations are already up everywhere."

"I know. Lots of shopping to do. By the way, Jude is coming for dinner. He is bringing someone."

"Is he?" Lars said nonchalantly, relieved.

"Yes. I figured that we could have a Thanksgiving feast."

"Certainly. Except we do not celebrate it here," he admonished.

"We do a little," she said, trying to persuade him.

"Right. Whatever. Should be fun," he responded.

"Please say that this is over and that you have realised that he is just a family acquaintance."

"Yes. Yes. I know. More than that," he mumbled.

"What's that?"

"Nothing."

She thought that he had gone through it and was done. She changed the subject. They had dinner.

Chapter 13

Preholiday Cheer

The winter air had set in. Amelie and Lars wrapped up as they entered the car and then drove to the restaurant in Mayfair.

Jude and his new girlfriend, Monica, were waiting at the table and sipping an aperitif before the meal. The last time that he had been at the restaurant was over the summer. He recalled Nick and Hank. This was a more intimate affair with a special friend.

"Are you comfortable, dear?" he asked.

"Yes, thank you. This is a lovely restaurant. It must mean a lot to you."

"I know. I was here last with the Mullburys, and we had a lot to discuss and overcome. I am so happy that there is light at the end of the tunnel regarding that situation."

"From what I do know, it must have been tough for you all."

"Yes. I am glad that they trusted me, as it all could have gone the other way. We are all friends now and have been friends for a long time. Only more recently with Amelie. However, I still consider her family."

"I cannot wait to meet her. She must be remarkable," she acknowledged.

"Yes, she is more than you would think. She does not realise the strength that she has sometimes."

"I am sure that you remind her."

"I do; however, it is hard to get involved with her personal life. I sense that her husband would not understand."

"I see. Well, we get to meet them again tonight."

Amelie and Lars rushed in, a little late because of the traffic, and headed to the table.

"Hello, hello. Sorry that we are late," Amelie said, ecstatic.

"Yes. There was traffic. Lots of shoppers must be on the road," explained Lars.

"Hello. It is lovely to see you," Jude greeted Amelie with a hug.

"Lovely to see you," she replied. "Hello. I am Amelie, and this is my husband, Lars," she said, directing her attention towards Monica.

"Hello. So wonderful to meet you both."

"Likewise," said Lars as he shook her hand and then shook Jude's hand.

"Hello, Lars. Great to see you again. We were just having a drink before you arrived."

"Yes. Shall we order something?" he asked Amelie.

"Please. The usual," she replied to her husband.

"Fantastic. Merlot?"

"Yes, darling."

He motioned the waiter, who took more drink orders and brought the water.

"Fantastic. So did you have a pleasant trip?" Lars asked.

"We had a wonderful trip, yes. Thank you," answered Jude.

"Great. So how are you enjoying London?" Amelie asked.

"It is lovely. I have always liked this city," Monica answered.

"I see. Where are you from?" she asked.

"Zurich. We met at the end of the summer in Zurich."

"Well, that is fabulous. We only just saw you this summer," she responded inquisitively.

"Yes, it was after that whole ordeal. My life just turned around," Jude explained, smitten.

Amelie grew more suspect the happier he looked.

"Really? Well, we are so happy for you both."

"Yes, really pleased. Why don't we make a toast to them?" said Lars.

"Sure." Amelie raised her glass.

"To Jude and Monica, and good friends, and a wonderful evening," Lars said.

"Hear! Hear!" answered Jude as they clanked glasses lightly.

"Hear! Hear!" followed Amelie and Monica.

"Where are you staying?" Amelie asked.

"At the Ritz, Amy," Jude answered.

"That's lovely. How are you liking that?"

"I love it. It is beautiful. We have a lovely view of the park."

"I know, it is a fabulous hotel. We have had dinner there," added Lars.

"Well, if you would like to meet for dinner there before we leave, we can," offered Jude.

"That would be smashing," said Amelie, enthused.

"Marvellous," said Lars. "Now let us see what they have. It looks like a winter menu with the squash salsa and beetroot soup. A nice hearty meal for a cold evening. I do not know where this year went. Last time we met, it was the end of the summer—I had to travel for business—and now the holidays are around the corner."

"I know. You must travel often. The summer moved quickly, and the case is finalised," observed Jude.

"Well, not that often any more," Lars said, looking at Amelie.

"Not as much, no," she agreed.

"As for the case, it is wrapping up. There is still more of a situation with the bank," Lars said.

"Yes, the bank," acknowledged Jude.

"I know. But almost over," concluded Amelie.

"Yes, Amy, almost over," added Lars.

"Great. Now for the main?" she asked.

"I think the pasta looks good," answered Monica. "I am not much of a meat eater."

"I figured. Which is why I selected this place."

"I will just have the seafood," added Jude.

"Fine choice. So shall I," said Lars.

"Jude tells me that you are in the travel business," Monica said.

"Yes. I was an estate agent until this whole mess, and now I manage property and exotic and sustainable trips for people. It is quite fun actually."

"Yes. You do have a nice array of clientele," Lars answered as he sipped his sherry.

"I think that it is amazing. You can plan a trip for us. We want to go to Hawaii," Jude said.

"Hawaii. Sounds marvellous."

"I know. I have never been, and Monica has friends."

"I see," added Amelie, sensing that this would be a very special trip for them. "When do you plan to go?"

"We would like to go in February for spring break," Jude answered, using air quotes.

"Yes. I will be going with friends from university," Monica responded.

"I see. I can arrange that for you. Just send me your preferences."

Lars looked away. He thought that this would be a fly-by trip; however, it was turning into a bit more.

"That should be wonderful, dear. We are planning our trips for the holidays ourselves."

Amelie looked at Lars. "Yes. We are going to Nan's, and then we are going to New York to see Dad and Nadia. She will be performing in February."

"Fantastic. We shall cross paths then," observed Jude.

"What a coincidence," added Lars.

The waiter brought the main course, and the couples consumed their feast. Amelie felt as though she was in her element and grew to like Monica, who had a very sophisticated and reserved demeanour. She was almost like her. Jude had chosen very carefully. Monica was very determined that she would be in his life for quite some time.

"Do you ski, Amelie?" Monica asked.

"Yes. It has been awhile, hasn't it, darling?" she asked Lars.

"Yes." He nodded.

"Great. We go to a lodge in March. You should join us."

"That is wonderful. We would be delighted."

"Given, of course, my workload. We will have made two trips for the year already, dear," added Lars.

"Yes. We will see. But thank you."

"Yes, I want to take Jude. It is close to where I grew up, and I would go with family," Monica added.

Amelie thought that it was a bit too soon to be so forward.

"Oh. Do you see much of your family now?"

"Well, my parents died in an accident when I was in college in the States. It is just my sister and me really."

"I am so sorry," Amelie lamented.

"I know. Do not worry. It usually comes up in conversation. I moved back to Switzerland to run the family business. Now I have finally found someone after all that pain."

"That is great. I am so happy for you both," Amelie said.

"Yes, so sorry to hear that. We will think about it," added Lars.

"That would be very nice of you if you could come along," added Jude, now that Monica had revealed her tale.

"This is a wonderful platter. How is your pasta?" asked Lars.

"It is fine, thanks," responded Monica.

"Great. And you, Amy?"

"Wonderful," she said while trying to chew.

"You, Jude?"

"It is a fabulous choice."

"Great."

There was so much in common between them as they discussed their lives in greater detail. It was the meeting of old friends and new ones. Lars would have to acquiesce to the idea that Jude might become a staple in their lives. It did not seem as though he would turn his back on the friendship with his wife and her family once more.

After dessert they parted ways. Jude and Monica returned to their executive room at the Ritz.

"I quite like Amy. I think that she is so sincere and full of integrity," Monica observed.

"Yes. I knew her mother very well. She has been through so much. Like you. She had a very hard time when her mother passed, I heard. She took forever to marry him."

"I see. I do not want to judge. I have been there too. Really, it takes a while. But now I have you. Our times have been wonderful, just wonderful," she commented.

"I am so happy that I found you too. I had so many questions about my family's dealings, and then there was this ordeal with the case. I am just glad that everyone is still on my side."

"I know, Jude. I know."

"Shall we order some champagne and celebrate life?"

"Yes. It is still early," she replied.

"What do you think?" Amelie asked Lars on the way home.

"Think?"

"Think of Monica. What do you think of Monica?"

"Oh, she is fab. I mean, I am happy for them," he answered sincerely. He truly was relieved.

"Yes. I think so. We should try to go in March."

"I guess. Depends on work, dear," he answered.

"Yes. You are right." She appeased him this time and thought that she would give it some time before addressing the issue again.

"I'm exhausted. I think that I will go over some work and then get some rest. It has been a long day." He made his excuses.

"Sure, I will be right up. I just want to leave some instructions for Marietta. I have a shopping list a mile long."

The holidays were fast approaching, and there was Granny's hamper and gifts for her father and Hank's children that she wanted to buy. She also wanted to get the cottage ready for the holidays. She and Lars would only manage to have a short break before heading to the island for the New Year. It would be a cosy country Christmas, after the traditional Boxing Day feast with Nicholas and Christmas Day with Aunt Marguerite.

"It is going to be a special Christmas with Uncle Lance's recovery."

"Yes. A special Christmas."

"What do you think your mother would like?" she asked.

"Well, she is not that bothered, is she?"

"No. I guess not. She likes those beaded sweaters for the holidays," she said, again to appease.

"Yes. That would be lovely."

Now, Amelie thought to herself, *what about Jude and Monica?* She did not want to go overboard as they'd only become reacquainted. It seemed that she would be a staple in his life.

"Yes. Anyway, there is so much work before then. I will be right up, dear."

She took out her notebook and listed a few items and then followed him to the room. She readied her Kindle for a long night of reading.

Jude sent a note the following day thanking them for the lovely dinner and expressing his hope that he'd see them all again. It was quick and to the point. Amelie did not know what to think of it all.

Amelie had a small party for the office. They all met for drinks after work the last Friday before Christmas. It was 21 December, and the weather had turned a blustery cold. She, Melanie, Delianna, and Teddy met at Ye Olde Swan, a popular place, and had drinks and dinner with mulled wine and holiday treats.

"Now, just because we are closing early on Monday does not mean that we are off call. Mr Mitchvale is still travelling, and the new arrangements are for Japan. Also, we have to ensure that Nadia is all straight for the New Year. I will be on call 24/ 7 from Nan's."

"Of course," agreed Delianna.

"Certainly," chimed in Teddy.

"Fabulous. I have so enjoyed this special time. Before we know it, it will be the first week of January. I have a bit of an extended holiday as we will be in New York to visit Nadia."

"Of course, we have it all under control," promised Delianna.

"I know that you do. This will be like all the other holidays."

"Definitely," added Teddy.

"Are you away this weekend?" asked Melanie.

"Yes. I am, actually. Then we have dinner with my aunt the following day with my dad. Has anyone verified if Lydia can make it?"

"Yes. She said that she and Manny will be there," reassured Delianna.

"Fabulous news. I will give you all your bonuses on Monday—just to ensure that you show up. Then there will be Christmas Day. Anything special planned for any of you?"

"I am going to Mother's in Lincolnshire," replied Delianna.

"Yes. I will just spend time with family here," added Melanie.

"Same here," added Teddy.

"We have a small gift for you. We all chipped in," offered Delianna.

"Thank you for a wonderful year," added Teddy.

"Yes, thank you."

"This is so lovely. Thank you," Amelie said, looking at the wrapped gift endearingly.

"You can open it on Christmas Day," Delianna continued.

"Right then. I will wait," Amelie replied, placing it next to her handbag.

"So more cheer, anyone?"

"Sure. Why not?" responded Teddy.

Amelie did not want to stay out late as she and Lars had an early country ride to the Cotswolds.

"My, I must be going. You all stay a bit longer. I will settle this bill," she ordered. "We have a long day tomorrow, and I have not packed. This week will fly by."

"Yes. That is all right," answered Delianna. "Thank you for the meal and drinks," she continued.

"Thank you. It has been lovely," added Melanie.

"Yes, thank you. And see you Monday," replied Teddy jokingly.

"Bye. Cheers." She left, wanting to be home when Lars arrived.

It would be one of the few remaining Fridays at the flat before the New Year. They never were able to enjoy it much. Mildred had helped with the tree again. It stood in the centre of the sitting room, asserting its creative presence. Amelie liked to turn the lights off and sit and stare at it. There were so many nostalgic ornaments. She rushed home to prepare for Lars's imminent arrival.

He arrived to dimmed lights and a sparkling tree. She had placed some cinnamon cappuccino on the tables with ginger cookies.

"This looks amazing," he said as he clambered, exhausted, onto the couch next to her.

"We needed something a bit magical to get us in the holiday spirit."

"I know. I suppose a lovely concert would do."

"Don't worry. I understand that you have a lot of work."

"We could still arrange something next week."

"We have so much to do. We fly next Friday, and the holidays are upon us, dear."

"All right. Why don't we play a few?"

He adjusted the player. Nat King Cole was the first to be played. Amelie nestled closer to Lars as they slowly sipped their coffee.

The following morning they loaded the four-wheel drive with their overnight bags and headed to Gloucestershire. It was a frosty morning, and the car was warm and cosy.

"It is a good thing that we have beat the rush," she opened the conversation.

"I know. We would have been crawling down the road in an hour or so."

"What would you like this year?" she asked.

"I don't know. Something technical, I suppose."

"OK. I will keep it as a surprise."

"Have you gotten something for your father yet?"

"Yes. Marietta picked up the usual on Jermyn Street. He is so easy to shop for as he is not that particular."

"Are you saying that I am?"

"No. I am just saying," she replied, bewildered.

They played some upbeat music until they arrived at their quaint driveway. They saw Nestor and waved as they pulled up. The flowers were no longer in bloom, and the pathway was lined with spiny sprigs. There was a country wreath with acorns and holly placed on the door.

"This is a lovely wreath," noted Amelie.

"Yes, Mrs Faverer, I thought that you would like it. I saw it in the storage room."

"Yes. It fits the season. Have you got the fireplace crackling?"

"Yes, ma'am. It is nice and warm for you. It is a bit frosty this morning, I have some groceries in the pantry. Also, the horses are ready, but the ground has to defrost a bit."

"Perfect."

"Yes. Thanks, Nestor," added Lars as they pulled their gear out the van.

"I have not seen Polka and Velvet in ages," Amelie said ecstatically.

"Yes, they are ready and expecting you."

"Great. We shall have a ride after lunch."

They entered the cottage and placed their boots at the entrance. Amelie wandered around and rubbed her hand on the wrought-iron fireplace.

"It is nice and warm in here. Darling, can you get us some coffee, please? We can have it in this room."

Before even running to the bedroom, Amelie plopped on the large settee and waited for her warm drink.

"Coming right up, dear," announced Lars. He enjoyed just the two of them and taking control at the country home.

He entered with two mugs of coffee and some more biscuits. "Nestor found these in town at the bakery."

"Lovely. Thank you, darling. Is there only *Snookers* on the telly?"

"No. There must be something on cable. I feel like a nice thick ploughman's and chutney relish. There is some thick home-made bread in the pantry."

"Sure, you can make it. Would be lovely with some tea."

"I love pampering you."

"Yes, dear. I love it too," she answered. "Right. We need to go riding after lunch. I think I'll ride Polka."

"Fine, dear. Whatever you would like. How about a night in the town? We have not been. I am sure our friends must be having some holiday cheer at the pub."

"Yes, darling. That would be all right. A nice country holiday meal."

"Right then. I will go and make the sandwiches."

"Thanks, dear. I will do a bit of unpacking. See you in a few minutes." Amelie finally got up and went to the bedroom. It was still cosy and filled with her cream decor contrasting with the dark beams. She took her toiletries out from the overnight bag and placed them on her vanity. She prepared herself for a lovely weekend full of country rides, walks, and village cheer.

After lunch, they took the long-awaited afternoon ride. Amelie mounted Polka, while Lars rode Velvet. They began a slow walk and then a light trot through the trail on the grounds.

"Careful of the trees. They have overgrown," Lars cautioned.

"I know. They are spiky too."

"The leaves have all fallen now."

"Want to canter?"

"No. Why don't we wait until it clears? I do not want to get scratched."

Lars stood a few inches taller than Amelie and was facing more sprigs.

Amelie pet Polka's mane as she hastened.

"Whoa," she said as she pulled the reins. "I think she wants to bolt."

"Yes. It has been awhile. She has to get used to you again," he replied.

"She knows me."

"I know." Lars did not want to get into it. He enjoyed the romantic ride with Amelie.

"Is this the way?" she asked, feeling a bit lost.

"It looks to be. Maybe it is the long way. Do not worry. The horses know the way."

Amelie turned around. "I am not sure. I think we must be lost."

"OK, Let's try to find the main road and get back from there. We might have taken a wrong turn. It would be chaotic if we got lost for the holidays."

"Yes. Let's turn here." They turned and rode until they were parallel with the road, at which point they tried to find their way back.

"What a relief," Lars said as they found their bearings.

"Great. We can canter now that we are out in the open," Amelie ordered.

"Yes."

They picked up the pace and rode at full speed for a few minutes. She slowed to catch her breath.

"I think that I might be a bit out of shape," she admitted.

"There is nothing like a ride out to get you back into shape."

They rode side by side until they got to the stables, where they dismounted. They patted the horses' necks and gave them some vegetables as a treat.

"Such a good girl," Amelie said while stroking her house. She missed the horses every time that she and Lars were in the city, and she relished the time in the country. "Shall we get ready for this evening then?"

"I am a bit knackered," Lars replied.

They rested and then got into the vehicle to drive to the pub in town. They walked into the cosy pub and sat at a table in the corner to have dinner. They were close and almost snuggling as their meals were brought. They sipped cinnamon drinks.

"Lovely. Just what I needed," Amelie expressed.

"I know. Just what we need. A lovely hot meal on this freezing night."

"It's not so cold with you here."

"No, not so cold," he responded as he drew her close and tucked into his meal. The two kept warm by cosying up together close to the fireplace. Laughter and festive music could be heard in the background. After a decadent dessert, they made their way back to the house.

Chapter 14

Yuletide Cheer

The festive feeling fuelled Amelie and Lars's ride from London to Surrey. They had an early start and entered the gates of the mansion by noon. She wore a red cashmere sweater and silk slacks. He was dressed in a grey shirt and navy tie.

"Here we go again. Another holiday at Aunt Marguerite's," she commented as they parked in the driveway.

"Yes. Another holiday. I will get the gifts from the back."

"Absolutely. Thank you, darling."

They rang the bell. Mildred answered. She was a staple at the holidays and had helped to prepare the meal.

"Hello. Happy Christmas!" she exclaimed.

"Happy Christmas! Are we the first ones?" Amelie responded.

"Yes."

"Happy Christmas, Mildred," added Lars.

"Happy Christmas to you. You can set those under the tree," she said, nodding towards the gifts. "Your aunt will be right out."

"Thanks. How have you been?" asked Amelie.

"Fine, thanks. We have been preparing all morning."

"It smells delicious. And the house is lovely as always."

"Thank you." The doorbell rang again.

Hank, Jasper, Jenny, and Hannah entered once Mildred had opened the door. She was pleased to see them. "Happy Christmas!"

"Happy Christmas!" answered the children as Hank and Jenny greeted her with a hug.

"Happy Christmas, Millie," responded Hank.

"Amy and Lars have arrived, and your aunt and uncle will be out shortly."

"Thanks. We will just head to the living room and unload these parcels under the tree," answered Jenny.

"Go straight ahead," Mildred answered. She had been assisting the family for the holidays her entire time with them. She was a close friend of Margaux, who included her in all the family preparations. Her extended family were all up north, and she'd never had children of her own.

Lance and Marguerite appeared in the living room and greeted the family with festive wishes. She wore a cream cashmere cardigan set and black satin slacks. It was tradition to spend Christmas with her as it kept the memory of their mother alive. There was the traditional goose and stuffing as well as plum pudding, a yule log, and minced pies. Marguerite would set out the fudge for the children and the stuffed stockings to play with until they could open their presents under the tree after lunch.

"We'll open those later," Marguerite promised the children as they relocated to the dining room. The table was set with her finest china and crystal.

"Sit anywhere, dears. We are not that formal this year."

"Yes, dear," answered Lance, who was recovering from his illness.

"Uncle, you are looking much better," noticed Amelie.

"Thank you, Amy. It has been a long recovery, but I am thankful that you are all here."

"Well, we are happy to be here and to be with you," she answered.

"Yes, Uncle. We would not want to be anywhere else," added Hank.

"Lovely to see you, Uncle," added Lars.

"Yes. The children were also so excited to come," Jenny said. "Do you need help with anything in the kitchen?" she asked her aunt.

"No, dear, we are fine. We are just adding the finishing touches and carving the turkey," responded Marguerite, who wanted this year to be perfect and had been up all evening preparing.

"It smells delicious, Auntie," added Hank.

It was important to have it just right as she'd thought that she would be lonely this Christmas, but then a miracle had happened. She and Mildred placed the plates in front of the family as they took their places at the table. Lance said the grace.

Marguerite started with a toast to her family and her late sister, as she always did. The family enjoyed their feast and sat and talked at the table until dessert. Mildred brought out the flaming plum pudding and served it with brandy butter to the adults. The children preferred the yule log and ice cream. The sunlight had dimmed, and Marguerite lit scented candles and played her carols as they all sat around the tree and sipped holiday coffee and opened the gifts. It was a chilly evening. The fireplace crackled as they shared in the delights of their gifts.

Lars and Amelie had another stop before heading back to London, so they decided to leave early. They would spend the evening with Lars's family, not far away, and then make the cheerful drive back to Knightsbridge.

Amelie bid her family farewell, promising to see Lance and Marguerite in the New Year on Epiphany upon her return from the island. Marguerite usually spent New Year's Eve in France at the chateau.

Marguerite had moved on from the dreadful news three years ago about the paintings. It had been another testing year, and they were still together to share it.

"Bye, darlings," said Marguerite. "Have a happy holiday and New Year. We will see you soon."

"Bye, Auntie, Uncle. Bye, Hank. See you all tomorrow at Dad's," Amelie answered.

"Bye-bye. Have a happy holiday and New Year!" said Lars as they left with their own gifts from family.

They drove to his home just near Slough. It was a more formal affair where his family had on cheerful and festive attire by the evening to open gifts and greet guests.

They had more dessert and coffee and then left for the smooth ride back to the flat. They arrived back at about 8 p.m. and sat and cherished their own tree. Christmas shows were on the telly, and then it was a restful night. They readied for the Boxing Day feast at Nicholas's favourite restaurant. Sitting by the fireplace and listening to the player while sipping tea took Amelie back to the magical days in the flat with her family during the holidays.

Amelie awoke feeling less stressful about the next day. It was simple to get to Mayfair, and there was no real kitchen work, just arranging the Christmas gift opening and dessert with friends afterwards. She and Lars had invited Orry and his wife as well as Lydia. So Nicholas's flat would be full for the evening cheer.

"What time do you have, dear?" Amelie asked, barely able to open her eyes.

"It is almost nine. We have had a little lie-in," Lars replied.

"We should leave here at about 12.30. I am not too bothered."

"Right then. Breakfast?"

"Who's cooking?"

"Well, we can just make some shakes or French toast. Not too much trouble. I will do it."

"Thanks, dear. Just a green shake for me."

"Lovely. Coming right up."

She peered out the window. It was a bit frosty, and she could feel the chill through the window. The seasons had moved on from summer, and she felt completely healed from that dramatic episode.

Lars returned with the shakes. "Do not get up, dear. Breakfast is served."

"Thank you, darling. Tastes delicious."

Nicholas was seated in his den, dressed in a tweed jacket and a burgundy silk scarf with wool trousers and a white buttoned shirt. He was going through his cards to hand out to his family. There were smaller gifts as the life of a semiretired man did not afford the extravagance that he once enjoyed. He only did minor consultancy.

Nadia was dressed in a sparkling black jumpsuit. She appeared the star that she was and was counting the days until her relocation in a few weeks to New York. Mildred was in the dining room setting out the teacups and dessert cutlery for after lunch.

"Dear, do you need anything? They should be here any minute," Nadia said to Nicholas.

"No, darling. I will just wait. Have you placed the youngsters' gifts under the tree?"

"Yes, dear. We will be out here. Mildred is just getting the china ready for the dessert," she said, implying that they were waiting for him.

"Coming right out," he replied as he counted his envelopes, ensuring that he had not forgotten anyone.

The doorbell rang. Amelie and Lars were coming up the lift. The doorbell rang again as Hank and his family followed. Nicholas waited in the sitting room as they all filed in for a quick toast before lunch. They would return and have a cocktail and dessert gathering with one of his oldest friends and his wife, and Lydia and her husband.

"Hello, Father. Merry Christmas," Amelie greeted him.

"Thank you, Amy. Merry Christmas."

"Mr Mullbury, happy holidays. Happy Boxing Day!"

"Thank you, and the same to you. How was yesterday?"

"Great. We had a splendid time, and Uncle is on the mend. He looks well."

"Fantastic," he answered. He always felt a bit left out and understood that his life had taken a different direction since Margaux had passed.

The doorbell rang again. Hank and his family entered with the children, who were eager to see their grandfather. They covered him as they jumped on his knees to wish him a happy Christmas.

Mildred popped in her head from the dining room, where she was setting up the drinks and cakes.

"Hello, dears. We are just in here preparing the cakes and some floating meringues."

"Did not see you over there," admitted Amelie.

"Happy Christmas, Amy, Lars," added Nadia as she entered the room to greet the family. She hugged everyone and showed the children their presents.

"Shall we unwrap these now?" teased Nicholas.

"Yes. Please," answered Hannah.

"Right then. Let's start. The reservation is at one o'clock," advised Nicholas.

"Perfect."

"Here you are, Hannah, Jasper," stated Jenny as she positioned herself under the tree.

They unwrapped with such haste and opened boxes to find electronic train sets, toy cars, and more Barbies with furnishing and clothes.

"We got those new dolls from the new FAO Schwarz over Thanksgiving," Nicholas proudly stated. "Do you remember that, Amy?"

"Barely, Dad. Sorry," she apologised.

"I remember," said Hank. "Amy would try to sit on the floor of the elevator as the elevator went to the top floor."

"Gosh, you do have a good memory," observed Amelie.

"Yes. I remember those trips," he said before he stopped, because he didn't want to state what was really missing.

"That sounds so sweet," added Lars.

"Right then. Are we all ready? It is just a short walk around the corner. The restaurant is waiting. We will see you in about two hours. I should think it should not be any longer than that."

"Right then, We are off." They all picked up their coats and set out to lunch.

By the time they returned, it was getting darker. The guests were meant to arrive at four. Orry and Cynthia arrived faithfully with parcels in hand. Lydia and Emani arrived shortly after. Also, a colleague of Hank's who was in town from Sydney, Geoffrey, and who was alone for the holidays joined them.

Mildred had champagne and soft drinks in glasses, ready to be served as everyone arrived. She had sliced some of the cakes and they were set on the dining room. The bowl with the meringues was on the counter with the sauces at hand.

"It all looks so perfect," remarked Lydia. "We are so excited to see you. It has been ages."

"Ages. We should not let that happen again."

"No. Well, Manny and I are off on a winter break to Sardinia," she informed her.

"Fabulous. We leave the day after tomorrow for the island. You need to come again. You have not been since the wedding."

"I know. But we are off to see his family. There are not enough days of the year."

"So, Orry, did you have a nice Christmas?"

"Splendid. The children came in, and we had a very large meal. So we are rather grateful for this invitation after the meal."

"I thought as much. Have some more drinks, Cynthia. Are you OK?"

"Yes, thanks," she answered, still feeling the strain since Margaux had left.

"I see. Well, how is business?"

"Fabulous," answered Orry.

"Great. You know all that mess is finally sorting itself out. Thanks for the tip, good friend. It was in the right direction."

"That is good to hear. He had such a reputation that the minute I heard it, I knew there was something wrong."

"There was so much more than that. It was the tip of the iceberg. There should be a case hearing early next year. The culprits are not able to do anything, so no more heists."

"Good to know that we are ending the year on a great note."

"That is right. Not too loud, or else Amy will hear. She had such a time with it all."

"Poor dear," empathised Cynthia, who was always concerned for Amelie's well-being.

"OK, dessert, I think. Will you have some dessert?" suggested Nicholas.

Hank introduced Geoffrey to the group. He was really a good friend who struck up a conversation with Lars over some old case on which they had been working. Pleased that they had something in common, they chatted for a considerable amount of time.

"Amy, the meringues are over here," Nadia offered.

"Thank you, Lydia. Let's have something for our bikini figures in the sunshine," she joked.

"Oh gosh. I cannot afford to lose mine. I am hoping for good weather."

"I as well."

"Here, dears," offered Mildred.

"Thank you. Always so tasteful," she commented.

"Thank you."

"We have to catch up in the New Year when I am back."

"Sure. We always say that." Lydia was aware of the breach between them and wished for a closer year.

"Plans always get in the way. Don't they?"

"Yes. They sure do."

The party went on until late, with everyone saying goodbye at nine. Once again, Nicholas was honoured to entertain such a good crowd for the holidays. There would be travel ahead, and the ecstatic feeling would not come around for another year.

"Another party over, dear," he commented to Nadia as they picked up the final bits.

"Yes. It was so lovely today as always. I am so relieved to have this week off."

"I know. The show must go on as they say."

"The show must go on. So the girls are coming for a few days to the island, and then it's back for a few rehearsals before the Big Apple."

"Time does fly. It certainly does, dear."

"You will be there for opening night, won't you?"

"Yes, of course. I wouldn't miss it for the world." He started to think about how to make the weeks in New York useful. "I suppose that I could meet a few contacts while I am there. It has been awhile."

"Lovely. It will be like starting afresh."

"Yes. Like starting over again."

"We are all so excited about New Year's Eve. ... Darling, there is space at the table for us all, right?"

"Yes, dear. I have it sorted. Mum and Dad prefer quieter evenings now. There is room at a table for ten with our six and the cast added."

"Fantastic. I truly can't wait."

"Splendid. How about an espresso?"

"That would be lovely."

They sat on the leather settee and sipped their coffee in front of the tree. "Another winter's holiday over."

"Another holiday over." She relished the thought of warmer weather in a few days.

Amelie had an overpacked bag on her way to the island. It was usual for her as it was packed with gifts for her grandparents and staff.

"Are you almost ready, darling? The car is coming in a few minutes."

"Yes, dear. Just sending this last email. The internet can be so unreliable in the tropics."

"Oh, it has gotten better. Have you everything?"

"Yes. Everything." He was accustomed to her minor anxiety.

"Good. I can hear the car."

"Fabulous. I shall just get the bags out. My, what is in here?"

"Lots of gifts for Gran."

"Wonderful," he responded. He enjoyed the New Year with her family. He had been travelling for a very long time.

It was a smooth drive to Heathrow. They disembarked and toted the luggage to check-in, where they cleared security and met her family in the lounge. The children were still half asleep while Nicholas and Hank drank their morning coffee.

"A bright and early morning, Amy," observed Nicholas.

"Yes, a bright and early one. How are you Hank, Jenny?"

"Fine. We are here and ready for a nap on the flight," responded Jenny.

"Yes. It is always worth it though," added Hank.

"I know. Mum is excited again."

"So are we," added Amelie.

"Hello. I see you have arrived," Nadia greeted as she arrived with a yoghurt and more coffee.

"Aren't you going to have something?"

"Just a little," replied Amelie as she looked at Lars. He nodded in reply.

"Great. I will get something."

"Thanks, dear. Just some juice and a cookie."

"Coming right up," he replied.

"It's just so hard to keep my stomach settled on the flight," explained Amelie.

"Oh dear," replied Nadia, agreeing.

They settled on the flight, taking up most of the club cabin.

"I think I will watch a film and get some rest," Lars indicated.

"Sounds good. I'll watch it with you," Amelie offered.

"If you wish. I do not know if you'll like it."

"All right. I'll choose my own. Just thought it would be nice."

"Anything you wish."

They took the breakfast mimosa being offered. Amelie would only indulge with family on the way out.

"Nice," Nadia commented as she took a sip.

"Lovely. Will Chrissy, Annabelle, and Augusto be arriving tomorrow?"

"Yes. We will see them tomorrow night as planned."

"Perfect. Dinner is at eight," added Nicholas.

Jenny had settled the children in and sat opposite Hannah, while Hank sat opposite Jasper. They sipped pure orange juice, and the children played with the gifts they had received from the flight attendant. Hannah placed hers down and went on her mini tablet. Jenny looked at her husband and was grateful that the children had settled quickly and would be fine for the quick flight over.

Amelie awoke just before the plane landed. She and her family collected their belongings and disembarked. The car was waiting for them as they were a large group. Nicholas would see his parents before heading out to the villa. They would be having dinner with Bruce and Mel that evening.

"I can't believe that this is such a short trip for me," noted Nadia as they drove to the house.

"Don't worry, you will be back soon. It is only a jump away from New York."

"That's right, darling."

"Nan has wonderful lights up," observed Amelie.

"Yes. The house looks lovely as usual," added Jenny.

They pulled up into the driveway. Winifred and Lionel were seated on the porch.

"What a glorious sight!" Winifred exclaimed as they disembarked. "We have been waiting to finally see you all."

"Nan, happy holidays. We hope that you had a lovely Christmas," said Amelie.

"Yes. We had a lovely one. Happy holidays to you, dear, and you, Jenny. Look at how the children have grown. Do you see that, Lionel?"

"Certainly. Come and give me a hug," he said as they greeted him.

"Father, Merry Christmas and compliments of the season."

"Yes. Compliments of the season, my son."

"Mother, Happy Christmas!"

"Happy Christmas, dear."

"The house looks ever so lovely again," added Nadia.

"Thank you, dear. Happy holidays. We have been preparing and just got the outdoor lights up on the twenty-fourth," replied Winifred.

"Simon should be able to help with the bags."

"That is fine, Momma. We have it."

"You do? I can lift something," offered Lionel as Simon appeared.

"That is all right, Gran," said Hank. It's just our bags and Amy's. We are all right. Thanks, Simon."

"You mustn't hurt your back, Lionel," added Winifred.

They brought their bags in, and all passed through the living room and went up to their rooms. Amelie and Lars took the pool house, while Hank and his family overtook the upstairs suite with a connecting bath,

"Lovely tree, Nan," remarked Amelie. "I just love those ornaments."

"I know that you do. I promised you those ornaments years ago."

"Thank you, Nan."

Verena popped her head in from the kitchen. It was filled with many sweet and savoury aromas.

"Welcome back," she said.

"Happy holidays, Verena. Smells delicious as always. What are you making?"

"There is a roast in the oven and some mince pies and cream for later."

"Lovely. We are starving."

"Yes. Smells wonderful, Verena. Happy holidays," commented Hank. "The children are starving. We will back in a minute."

Nicholas and Nadia, pleased to see Verena again, chatted with her in the dining room. She was like a member of the family.

"We will save the plum pudding for New Year's Day, as well as the goose, stuffing, peas, and rice."

"Reminds me of when I was a boy."

"Yes. When you were younger," she added.

"What's that?" asked Winifred as she settled at the table for lunch.

"The aroma reminds me of when I was younger and would come home from school for the holidays. Mum would throw some great parties."

"Yes, Nick. They were the talk of the town for the holidays."

"People stayed good all year to get on the list," he joked.

"Well, I liked to invite all walks of life. My family has a long history on the island, and we got to know so many people."

"Yes. There was a dress code."

"There certainly was. If I dressed the house, then you should be properly dressed. It took a lot of time and effort."

"We had a good time those nights. All the food would be laid out on the table, and we would have the soup and the turkey with all the trimmings," added Verena.

"Yes. I remember those days. I remember my friends at Christmas. Many have left us now. It was a long time ago. But it still all comes alive at the holidays."

"The desserts were endless, Mummy."

"Yes. It was a full sit-down meal for everyone."

"It sure was," reminisced Nicholas.

"Jenny, we have some macaroni and cheese for the children."

"Wonderful. They love your macaroni and cheese."

"Also some fudge from the bakery," added Winifred.

"Mummy, you wore all those designer clothes. You would get my suits from New York. Do you remember?"

"Yes. I remember. They came from my boutique."

"Sounds so magical, Winnie," said Nadia.

"Those nights, the patio would come alive. Sometimes I can still hear the laughter. All those memories."

"Memories of Christmases past," added Nicholas.

"That's right, Christmases past. So where are you going tonight, Son?" asked Lionel.

"We are going to dinner with Bruce and Mel at the club. Sort of a preparty celebration as tomorrow night will be crowded."

"Sounds like fun. Have something now. Verena has been preparing all morning."

"Yes, it is all ready," she said as she brought out a few dishes for the buffet table.

"You can serve yourselves and have a seat," added Winifred.

"Great, Nan. I'll have some. Is there any mint sauce?" asked Amelie.

"Yes, also some home-made cranberry sauce, dear. Just as you like it," replied Winifred.

"Thanks, Nan. I'll have some."

There was much to catch up as they poured out the year's activities over a delicious lunch. Nicholas and Nadia were driven to their villa and took a romantic stroll on the beach before preparing for dinner. Life seemed crystal clear again. He looked at the horizon and wondered why he had ever left and mused on how lucky he was to be able to return. That evening they celebrated the end of the year with close friends in a friendly environment. They got an early night's sleep and prepared for the New Year's Eve bash.

Chapter 15

New Year's Bliss

Amelie awoke on New Year's Eve with the memories of three years ago, when the ordeal had started. Her aunt had discovered that there was an attempted sale of the paintings by someone who had stolen her mother's identity. It seemed that everything had been drawn from the past. She searched for her husband. Lars was up and exercising on the patio. She walked out towards him.

"How about a walk on the beach? Sort of to put the year behind us," he suggested.

"Lovely. I will just grab my jacket. It is a bit chilly, don't you think?"

"Yes. I think so. Can you get mine as well, please?"

"Sure, darling." She returned with the jackets and threw one around her shoulders.

"Shall we?" He offered his hand.

They took a long stroll as the waves crashed against the early morning shore. The sea was choppy, and the small boats bobbed up and down on the water. The sun rose to midpoint and would remain there until the end of the day. The day went slowly as they prepared for the bash that evening.

Amelie had a long navy-sequin-embellished gown set out to wear. It was a classic from her grandmother's collection. She felt sentimental and nostalgic and decided to g a bit vintage for the evening. Lars would wear his regular tuxedo. It was cosy getting dressed in the cottage, compared to their large high-ceiling flat in Knightsbridge. There was a mystical end of the year and an evening feeling in the air. The sun had set by 5 p.m. and left an orange-gold sky.

It was a time of reflection. Amelie thought of how much she had grown and overcome over the past year. She was still young at twenty-eight and had taken on professional responsibilities and built her own business. She was lucky enough to have her family, but still missed her mother during the holidays, especially at New Year's Eve when Margaux radiated and oozed glamour with whatever she wore. There were many memories. She would now continue the tradition.

The day passed quickly, as it does, and the afternoon sun grew dimmer and left a purple-red sky. The horizon looked mystical as the sea grew a deep blue and shimmered in the new moonlight. Amelie slipped on her heels as Lars tightened his tie.

"Any more thought on the ski trip in a few weeks?"

"No," he answered. "Why don't we think about it later?" He wanted the evening to be about them without any distractions.

"I know. Sorry," she replied. It was as if Jude would bring her closer to her mother.

"I think I know where this is going. You have so many people around you, especially Aunt Marguerite. How many more do you need to get over everything?"

"I have gotten over everything. I just think that it would be a nice gesture," she replied as she added her accessories.

"OK. We will think about it later," he conceded.

They walked to the main house and met Hank and Jenny, all dressed for the festivities of the evening.

"Such a lovely dress, Amelie," noticed Winifred.

"Really? Thank you. It is one of yours."

"Yes. We carried that. You look like your mother in that."

"I thought it was something that she would wear."

"Definitely. You all have a lovely time and a happy New Year. Be careful, of course, and we will see you for lunch tomorrow."

"Yes, Nan. See you tomorrow. And happy New Year to you both."

They arrived at the gala and sipped champagne with the other members of their table. Nicholas was with Nadia, who'd also invited Chrissy, Annabelle, and Augusto. Bruce and his wife met them and had a few drinks before heading to their group. The cast members provided a bit of mystique to the evening as the club members wondered who they were. Nonetheless, the champagne flowed and the band played as they were seated and continued their conversation about the move to the Big Apple and rehearsals. Jenny was thrilled and had a trip planned, as had Amelie.

"Shall we dance?" Hank extended his arm. He and Jenny walked to the dance floor.

Nicholas and Nadia followed with Chrissy and Augusto. Hank wanted to brush up on his waltz skills. Nicholas led the way with Nadia.

"We are planning a trip soon to New York. Are you done with rehearsals?" asked Amelie.

"Yes. But we have more," responded Annabelle.

"I can't wait to see the production again," Amelie said politely.

"Sure. Just let us know, and you can come backstage."

"That would be exciting," she responded, looking at Lars.

Taylor Sumpton approached the table and asked Annabelle for a dance. She responded amicably and continued to the dance floor. They were professional dancers and added extra flair to the entertainment. They were accustomed to being the centre of attention and worked very well together, which was evident on the floor. Neither upstaged the other as if they were still onstage.

Taylor had always had a keen eye for women. He also had an instinct regarding new arrivals to the island. He was also very wealthy, and visitors enjoyed his playboy lifestyle. He was made for entertaining, and the evening at the club was his forte. He continued to entertain Annabelle for the evening and revisited the table after the lavish meal for another dance. Ringing in the New Year with someone new was one of his resolutions.

Amelie stayed close to Lars as she usually did. His were the only arms she wanted to embrace at midnight. It was evident that no one would have been able to get in between the two of them. It was a lively New Year's Eve celebration that lasted well beyond the stroke of midnight. Many were still on the floor at 2 a.m. Amelie and her group decided that it was time to end the evening. There was a New Year feast at Nan's the following day.

"Dad, we are going to call it a night. What about you?"

"Yes, I think so. Happy New Year, Amy," he replied.

"Happy New Year. Are you coming tomorrow?"

"Yes. Only me as Nadia will be entertaining on the beach."

"See you then." She and Lars left via taxi for the short ride back to the house. Her grandparents were already asleep after having rung in the New Year in front of the telly. The couple were cautious as they headed to the back and then on to their cottage.

Marguerite and Lance were at the chateau in northern France, having spent a quiet New Year. She was simply relieved that he was still with her after the year that they had had. It was already New Year's Day. There was a crisp chill in the air, and the landscape was frozen. It would soon thaw as it was a very mild winter. She had the cook prepare a very traditional breakfast of eggs and potatoes, all from the vicinity. It was tradition for them to sit and enjoy another feast the following morning.

"It is such a fresh morning. The breeze is cool. Have you enough on, dear?"

"Yes. I am fine. Do not worry about me."

"Are you sure?"

"Sure, dear. I will have some more fresh coffee."

"Here you go, darling." She passed it to him.

"Thank you, dear. Wonder what Nick and Amy got up to last night?"

"The same. An evening at the club, I would suppose. Margaux loved it. She was there every New Year's Eve. Such a socialite. She had so many friends on the island, and she was so fashionable."

"Yes. She was."

"I can't help but remember her during the holidays."

"I know, dear. I know."

Marguerite tried to digress and concentrated on the meal. The thyme and fresh herbs of the eggs added extravagance to the breakfast. The sautéed potatoes were crisp and drizzled with a bit of truffle and olive oil and sea salt.

"It is very tasty this morning."

"Yes. Very tasty." He seemed to agree with everything she said.

"We can relax in front of the fireplace. What is on the telly?"

"I do not know. There is always something good on New Year's Day."

Nicholas arrived at the house nursing a headache. He got a dubious look from Winifred, who could tell he was under the weather. It was if he were dragging himself in after a spring break evening while home from college. He was never too old to receive the look.

"Happy New Year, Mother," he murmured.

"Happy New Year, dear. Did you stay out late last night?"

"No, not too late. Nadia had colleagues down and sends her apologies."

"I see. We will miss her. Amy and Lars should be over soon. Jenny is taking care of the children."

"Hello, Dad. Would you like anything?" asked Hank.

"Yes. Just a Bloody Mary for now."

"Sure, coming right up."

"Happy New Year, Mr Nick," added Verena as she popped her head in from the kitchen.

"Same to you. What do you have for us today?"

"I have been in the kitchen all morning. All of your favourites."

"Smells delicious."

"That is right. We have vegetable pea soup and doughboy with plantain and pumpkins and some banana potato bread. There is a roast with mint sauce and some treacle pudding for dessert. There's also a nice lemon vanilla cake with royal icing."

"Sounds superb. Can't wait." A lovely stodgy meal was needed to take the edge off a beautiful evening.

"Mama, is anyone else coming?"

"Yes, my cousins, Rebecca and Wilmot. They were here last Boxing Day."

"I remember. Where is Amy?"

"She is resting. I could hear her and Lars up on the patio when they got back."

He smiled, remembering what it was like having New Year's with Margaux. Although feeling renewed, he also had nostalgia.

Winifred glanced at him as if to remember when the house was more alive.

"Is Nadia going out?"

"Yes. Her friends are with her, and they are going boating at the club. They have to leave tomorrow and prepare for the show in New York."

"Oh. Should be nice. However, the sea is a bit choppy today. Not a really good day for that."

"No. I suspect they will just enjoy the band at the bar on the beach."

"I suppose." She was reticent to express her real feelings. However, she wanted to see him happy, so there was no choice really. Nadia was from a different generation, and Nicholas was putting up with it.

"Don't worry. We can visit more from New York."

"I suppose. Verena, is my music playing?"

"Yes, ma'am. I will turn it up for you."

"Thanks." Winifred liked to play Bach on New Year's Day as the distinct melody was crisp and refreshing.

"Lunch will be in twenty minutes."

"Looking forward to it," replied Nicholas.

Amelie decided to place a call to France before lunch.

"Bonne année, Auntie!"

"Bonne année! Merci. Ca va?"

"Ca va."

"How did it all go last night?"

"It was beautiful. We had a superb time."

"Fantastic. Your mother always loved the galas. I do miss her."

"So do I. You should see the vintage gown that I wore. I will send you the photos."

"Lovely. I am sure that you looked lovely."

"Where is Uncle Lance?"

"He is resting, dear. We had a lovely night and a perfect lunch today. I suppose we shall have something light. He is recovering, and it looks like a wonderful year ahead with all the summer parties again, dear."

"What a relief that we have been so lucky."

"We certainly have. We shall have lunch when we get back after Epiphany."

"Sounds great."

"Bye for now."

"Bye, darling. And send my best to everyone, won't you?"

"I will."

She disconnected, relieved that the ordeal from two years ago was over and there was not a repeat of it this year. She was appreciative to her husband and his company for seeing it all through.

"She sounds pretty good. No need to worry."

"That's good."

"We had better wander over to Nan. There is a major lunch under way."

"Perfect," Lars replied.

"It should heal all ills."

"I know. That soup is spectacular."

"Just what we need to revive us."

The family had a hefty meal and enjoyed each other's company. Once again, they were seated where they could view the sea and the road below with cars heading out for a New Year excursion. They served themselves buffet style and enjoyed the savoury delicacy with all the sides and then dessert. The year had started at a normal setting, and they looked forward to continuing along that route.

The winter in New York was upon them. Nadia arrived mid-January and, still ensconced, plunged onto the large white sofa in her loft. There were high ceilings and a vacuous space. She took a nap before deciding to take a walk to pick up a few groceries. She found a specialty store with many European treats and ready-made rotisserie and sushi. She decided to buy as much as she could as her days would be spent rehearsing and preparing for the show in February. Nicholas was arriving in ten days, when hopefully the stress would be over and she would be more amiable. She took a taxi back to the apartment with her packages and was still knackered.

The phone rang. "Hello?"

"Hello. You have arrived. Welcome to the Big Apple," Anabelle replied.

"Thank you. Gosh, I am still a bit weary," she admitted.

"Aw. Wanted to see if you wanted to have dinner tonight?"

"I think I need a nap first. What time?"

"About sevenish?"

"I'll see. That would mean at about midnight."

"I know. I am just getting over the jet lag as well. I have had a few more days' luxury."

"Have you? What about the others?"

"They should all be here by the weekend. We do not have much time until rehearsals start."

"All right then. Phone me first to see if I am awake."

Nadia hung up and could sense the driver's prying eyes. She left the cab and took the lift up to the loft. There was a sense of liberation and that the city was now hers. It felt like a fresh beginning in the midst of the January wind, a fresh new year and filled with more possibilities. She had a view of the Hudson and could see the boats ferrying down the river as the sun grew dim. She closed the blinds, making the apartment dark and cosy, put on her eye mask, and fell asleep.

A bit later, she got a call. It was Anabelle. "Good Lord, what time is it?" Nadia asked, shocked.

"Six-thirty? Are you ready?"

"I am just getting up." She looked around the flat. The groceries were still on the kitchen counter.

"All right. What time do you think you will be ready? I am just heading to the restaurant on Forty-Eighth Street."

"Give me another half an hour. It is not that far from here."

"No. You are only about four blocks away."

"Right. I'll be there soon."

"See you."

She dragged herself up and freshened up. She was barely unpacked and left everything as she put on her cream coat and scarf.

Her phone rang again. It was her husband.

"Hello, darling. Are you all settled in?"

"Getting there. Just off to have dinner."

"Sounds lovely. Shall I call back?"

"It is a bit late. Let me call you in the morning."

"All right. Love you."

"Love you and miss you. Bye, darling." She hung up.

She walked four blocks in the cold New York air. The city was filled with people rushing to get home, whereas her evening was just beginning.

"Hello. You look great, considering," Annabelle greeted her.

"Hello. Lovely to see you. Thanks for inviting me. Sorry to be so sour. I am feeling a lot better after the nap."

"Wonderful. There is a table upstairs reserved. I just thought I would wait near the door."

"Thanks."

"Shall we?" Annabelle motioned to the hostess to take them upstairs, where they had a view of the street below.

"This is nice," Nadia commented. "Let's get some tequila cocktails."

"Ooh, let's. I do not know when we will get the chance again."

Anabelle looked around. "I have always liked the atmosphere. I was here with Augusto last year. Look where we are a year later."

"I know. There is so much work to do until we open."

"I know. Well, opening night shall be a real celebration."

"I just want to get through this weekend," Nadia answered despondently.

"Not to worry. You will. We all will—together, as we always do."

"Yes. I think so." Nadia was more optimistic as the evening wore on, but she was still very exhausted.

"Right, so Chrissy and Augusto arrive in the morning. We are all going out tomorrow night. Want to come along?"

"Maybe I should just rest."

"Come on. There won't be any more time before the show."

"All right. I will."

"Fabulous. Will send you the details."

"Great. Sorry, I just miss Nick."

"Aw. He will be here in no time. Two weeks, dear, and you won't know what to do."

"I am sure." She laughed.

"This part of town is so alive."

"You are right. The Theater District." She focused on the street below and thought of her cosy home in Mayfair on that quiet street.

"We should order soon."

"Yes. Let's."

Nadia managed to eat most of the platter of quesadillas and guacamole. Sadly, it was time to get some sleep and to say goodbye to the evening.

"See you tomorrow. Get some rest. I know that you feel dreadful. You will be in company with the others," noted Anabelle.

"I know. Thanks for being so understanding. But we have to end the evening so that I can get some rest."

"Cheers. We must bring the others here."

"Have a nice evening."

She jumped into a taxi and headed back to the loft, where the doorman hastily acknowledged her approaching and she stepped into the elevator. Her recollection was shady after that point and she ensconced herself into the large bed.

Two weeks passed, and Nadia was ready for opening night. Besides the aches and pains from rehearsal, she was in top form. Nicholas was set to arrive, and she had the apartment clean and decorated with a few flowers. She looked around. Finally the apartment would be alive. She remembered the last time that he was in the room and how grand he stood in comparison to everything.

The buzzer rang.

"Hello?"

"Yes. Mrs Mullbury, it is your husband, Nicholas."

"Thanks. You can send him up as he will be with me now for a few weeks."

"Certainly."

She ran to the door and opened it, waiting until she heard the ping from the elevator.

"Darling!" she exclaimed.

"Yes, dear." He rushed and embraced her.

"So wonderful. I have been waiting. Come in."

He entered with the same confidence he'd had the day he first walked in.

"I have been waiting too. Still looks marvellous," he said, noting the interior.

"What about me?"

"You too, dear. Of course you do. Actually, a bit slimmer."

"Really? We have been working out," she replied, pleased.

"Not enough scones."

"I suppose not."

"Chilly outside."

"Yes. There is meant to be a storm Sunday."

"Luckily it won't ruin your opening night."

"Yes. Early February can be a bore."

"It is cold in London at the moment."

"Really? I have not kept up."

"Oh yes. A real chill. But the heating in here is really good. The flat is a bit dated in that respect."

"Yes. But I miss the flat too. How is everyone?"

"Wonderful. Amy and Lars should be in soon. They are staying near the park. Lance is much better, and Hank is holding the fort until I get back."

"Lovely. I can't wait to see Amy and Lars. I am so happy that they made it to opening night."

"She is ecstatic to come. It had been awhile since she was last in New York. She is eager to see the place."

"I know. She helped us find it. And what a good job she has done."

"Yes. She is busy with work but can work from here. This is her little break."

"Great. We are so ready. You should see the production. You are going to love it."

"I know."

"Coffee? This is a brilliant machine. I got the Italian roast that you like."

"Yes. Certainly. That would be lovely. It is only about six London time. Are you hungry? I suppose we could go somewhere in the neighbourhood to get something eat."

"Splendid. Then I have rehearsal. I can't wait for you to see everyone tomorrow night."

"Truly. I would be delighted."

The pair caught up on two weeks of an absence. Nadia really hoped that Nicholas would stay the whole month. The production could go on, or it might not last. It depended on the sales and audience.

"I'll go and freshen up, and then we shall be on our way."

He still had lots of energy and decided he could relax later as he navigated his jet lag.

"This is a fantastic view. I love this suite!" said Amelie. "I love it. There is just something about the Big Apple. Mind you, I do not get to come enough for work."

"Now that is an idea. I have so many contacts that I could probably open a branch here one day."

"Yes, certainly. Let me know if you will need anyone to fill in?" Lars responded.

"What a wonderful concept. What is it about New York that makes you feel so ambitious when you land?"

"The feeling that you can make it."

"Yes, precisely," she pondered.

"It must be the vast sky and reaching for your goals."

"It must be."

"So are we ready for that walk?" he asked.

"Surely. I cannot think of anything more pending than to take a romantic stroll on a Friday afternoon down Fifth Avenue."

"Down the avenue ..."

"Fifth Avenue ..." she chimed in.

"Let's go, shall we?"

"Certainly. The clothes can unpack on their own."

"That's right. We can deal with that when we return. No chores here."

"None taken."

The street was bustling and crowded for a Friday. It was chilly. Amelie and Lars wrapped up in their scarves and large puffer jackets as they walked against the billowing wind.

"What a New York winter."

"It's freezing. Let's get some coffee."

They stopped at a place near Sixth and the park.

"I love it. There are so many tourists. I can really start a travel office here."

"You most certainly can."

"Thanks for that vote of confidence."

"I mostly have a continental practice from my qualifications. It would be difficult to start here."

"It would be difficult?"

"Yes, so many regulations."

"I see. Well, what about the case? Have you heard from Hank?"

"Yes. It is almost over, dear. Soon it will all be behind you, and it cannot follow you to New York."

"Thankfully. Here we are closer to Nan."

"Surely we are."

"Now, are we going to the French Alps with Jude and his new lady friend?"

"I think we will pass. This trip will be enough. It is already over a week and I have to get back. There is a new case I am starting in Spain."

"OK. Such a pity. I suppose that we will make the most of this one."

"Yes, definitely." He knew that she would come around. There was no way that he would spend any more time with Jude in that way. He wanted it to remain strictly professional regardless of the past.

"Are you warm enough? I think that we can wander into a shop and find a sale."

"Such a good time for bargains."

"Really?"

"Yes, and I need something for the club ball in May."

"It will be here before you know it."

"It always creeps up on you. The summer, I mean."

"Well, here's to another summer." He raised his cup.

"Yes, all the events. I love my season in the spotlight."

"Yes. Tomorrow will be a different type of spotlight at the theatre."

"That is right. An evening of bright lights and big city."

"Perfect. I cannot wait to see it. We must get a gift for Nadia."

"I know. She has been wonderful getting us tickets and a pass."

"Well, look at that swank suite you found her. You did your bit."

"I am sure that she is beyond gracious regarding that. I hear that she loves it."

"Let's hope not too much. She might not come home."

"Oh. The worst would be that Dad would spend time here. He tried to make a go of things when he was younger. That is how I know a little about the market here."

"I see. I like this area better." He looked around as they left.

"It is more traditional. Always wanted to wander and view a flat. That would be a good idea?"

"Shall we? I suppose that it would be all right."

"Yes. Let's take a look at a place around the park. There are such good schools around here."

"Just to look, dear. I cannot make promises."

"I know, just to look. Besides, how could I ever turn my back on that quaint, safe street that has always been my sanctuary?"

"I know, dear. And the homeliness of the environment after 3 p.m. with those lovely little ones being accompanied by parents and caregivers to their home."

"Yes. It really would be a different lifestyle. However, the world is so different. Is there really a safe place? And won't our family need to compete with that development?"

"I suppose. There is so much to think about. Besides, you would not want to miss the periwinkles in bloom."

"No. However, there must be some in April in New York?"

"Possibly."

They walked, striding arm in arm, until they found a department store. Amelie tried on several dresses until she found two which were 30 per cent off and a bargain with the exchange rate. Now she was certain that there would be no duplicates of her outfit at the gala.

"We should probably head back. I am tired all of a sudden."

"Certainly. I will go to the gym while you nap."

"Wonderful."

The blustery and chilly winter's breeze blew through them as they bundled up and, with their shopping bags, exited the store. It was darker out now. The afternoon was coming to a close.

"Why don't we have dinner on Top of the Rock at the Rainbow Room tonight?"

"That would be lovely."

"I'll see what the concierge can arrange."

Opening night was upon them, and Nadia was a little sore from the extensive rehearsing. The family would be arriving at 7 for the show at 7.30 and curtains at 10. She was preparing in her dressing room when she heard a knock.

"Just coming in to wish you the best of luck, dear." Nicholas approached with flowers.

"Thank you, darling. They are lovely!" she exclaimed as she turned to him in full character.

"It's a full house tonight. All to see my lovely wife."

"Is it? I have not had time to think," she replied, trying to calm the jitters.

"You'll be fine, dear," he soothed as he detected her reticence.

"Amelie and Lars send their best. She cannot wait for the after-show dinner. She has been looking forward to this for weeks."

"Send my best, and let her know that I really appreciate her coming."

"I will. And break a leg. Not literally of course."

"No. Thank you."

He turned and left. She felt that vacancy and realised that he was only a few steps away and that it was opening night and the show must go on.

Anabelle entered. "Are you all ready?"

"Yes. How are you holding up?"

"A bit nervous. What about you?"

"All right, considering. Look at those ... aren't they lovely?"

"Yes. Thank you. My fabulous husband just brought them in."

"Roses. My, what a dear."

"Yes. How are the others?"

"We are just about ready."

"Right. Let the show begin," answered Nadia as they exited the changing room.

The crowd applauded and applauded. Nadia could hear the echo of the applause and could see just silhouettes of faces in the audience. She detected her family and tried not to get too distracted as she concentrated on her lines and her steps.

Finally, there was curtain call. The show had ended. She returned and Amelie and Lars entered the changing room.

"That was wonderful. Thank you. We fully enjoyed it," commented Amelie as she greeted her.

"Wonderful. Thank you for coming."

"Our pleasure truly," she responded.

"Yes. Amy has been on about this for weeks. It was a fantastic show. I hope that it gets the reviews that it deserves," added Lars.

"I do hope so. Shall we all meet at Sardi's?"

"Absolutely. Dad's gone over to secure the spot. We shall be celebrating tonight," Amelie assured Nadia.

There were more knocks as Anabelle, Chrissy, and Augusto entered.

"I am so thrilled. Did you hear the crowds?"

"Yes, it was magnificent. So electrifying to hear them."

"It was a superb show. I am sure that it will do very well," commented Amelie.

"Yes, it will do very well," added Lars. "You put in so much work, and you all were superb."

"Thank you. Well, see you at the after-theatre dinner," replied Augusto.

"See you."

Lars and Amelie left to meet Nicholas and to order a few drinks before the stars arrived. It was a brilliant Broadway evening. The district was alive and pulsating with energy. It was very late in London, but they were revived by the atmosphere. The energetic pulse that revved through each soul invigorated them and the atmosphere. Sleep had checked out, and an awakening came in.

Nadia's face became one for the walls and marquees like those that covered the restaurant's wall. Photos were taken as the wine was poured and the plates were passed. There was the feeling of togetherness, the same feeling that had gotten them through the year. It had been a tough year, but one that Amelie had pulled through with the trusting help of the people around her—the people who cared for her and those that stuck beside her.

There was a new beat in the heart of the city, one that showed her that a person can overcome and that life can start again. There was laughter and a special camaraderie. Maybe there would be many more moments such as this, or perhaps there would not be any for a long time. Whatever the case, life was always changing, and there would be more that she would have to optimistically anticipate.

Printed in the United States
By Bookmasters